Steamy Stories

Stories From Steamy Springs

by Jennifer Kitt

Previously published separately as:

Hot Water
Unlawful Entry
Fertility Rites

Copyright 2012 by Jennifer Kitt

Hot Water

Chapter One

Katherine Chase drove her SUV along the narrow mountain road, rapidly climbing up and away from the town below. She looked down at the buildings in the distance and saw the steam rising from the hot springs on the valley floor. Snow was beginning to fall and she bit her lip nervously, hoping that the weather wouldn't get too bad, and that she'd be able to make it safely back again in the evening.

She wondered if Richard would be there. If he hadn't started out yet, the snow might prevent him from reaching the hotel, and given his schedule, if they couldn't sort out the unfinished rooms, it could set back the project another few months. He was off to Hawaii next week to work on a new beach-front hotel, and who knows when he'd be back.

She had to get the hotel finished and open by spring. They had been due to open *The Spa in the Clouds* in December, in time for the ski season, but an exceptional early snowfall had meant a series of delays. Everything had to be brought up by truck from Steamy Springs, which was, in turn, mostly supplied out of Denver. With one small mountain pass climbing up thousands of feet to the hotel, the winter weather was always going to present some problems. Still, it would be worth it. It was going to be the best little boutique hotel in the Rockies.

The hotel was Katherine's baby, and as she drove, she glanced at the images Richard had sent her. His revised designs for the rooms were spectacular, and since most of the interior architecture had been done and it was mainly a case of finishing and furnishing the remainder of it, the hotel would meet its new opening date. Some of the bespoke furniture, designed and made in Italy, was due to arrive next week. Looking at the designs made Katherine excited about the project again. The setbacks of the last few months and the delayed opening had stressed her out, and she was looking forward to getting the project finished, and taking a well earned holiday.

The Spa in the Clouds was her first solo project and, being a Chase, she had a lot to live up to. Her Grandfather and Father had developed the town of Steamy Springs in the valley below. From a single hotel back in the 1950s they'd turned it into one of the best holiday spots in the country. An all year round hot springs resort, with ski-ing in winter and mountain sports in summer. You name it, the Chase family had built it: hotels, spas, restaurants, lodges, sports facilities, they'd even carved out the pistes and built the ski lifts system.

Katherine and her three sisters had all been groomed from a young age to take over the family's business empire, and because she was the oldest daughter, she felt like *The Spa in the Clouds* was a way she could really prove herself. She hadn't received any help from her father, and had set about building her little outpost of the Chase family empire four thousand feet above Steamy Springs. A fantasy hotel set amongst the Rockies' loftiest peaks. She'd needed a good architect, of course. And she'd found one in Richard Ford. He specialised in exclusive hotels and spas, and although he worked out of a beautiful office overlooking Lake Tahoe, his work took him all over the world. Still only in his early thirties, he was fast becoming the guy to go to if you wanted to build your dream.

As she neared the hotel, Katherine felt a twinge of excitement. It was a familiar feeling. It always appeared when she was going to see Richard. She'd felt it the first time they met, when he accepted the job. A merry little flip-flop in her stomach, and a quickening of her heartbeat. They had spent many weeks together over the last two years, poring over plans and designs, and throughout all that time, nothing had happened. She wondered if Richard liked her. There was no reason why he wouldn't. She was twenty seven years old, body of a lingerie model, and a gorgeous face framed by long blonde hair. He'd once briefly mentioned a girlfriend in California, and she'd got the impression she was an Asian girl. Maybe he went for exotic looks.

She pulled up outside the hotel and, to her relief, Richard was already there. She got out of the SUV and ran over to his Porsche, the snow falling heavily. She gestured for him to go to the main entrance, and he got out and joined her.

"Hi Richard," she said, looking him up and down, and feeling the familiar urges come back. He was a great looking guy. Six foot, athletic, dark brown hair and intense eyes. He also had a deep tan. "You been somewhere hot?"

He touched the skin on his face and smiled. "Dubai. It's one hundred degrees out there most days. Way too hot."

"So you've come to Colorado to cool down."

"No. I've come to see you, of course," he replied.

Katherine was at a loss as what to say. She sometimes felt like a gawky teenager when she was with him, and usually said something dumb "Oh. Okay. Do you like what you see?"

Richard nodded. "Absolutely." He stared at her just a shade longer than he thought he probably should have. He couldn't take his eyes off her. She was stunning. She'd pulled up the hood of her white sheepskin jacket, the fur lined opening framing her face perfectly, and her hair falling down on to her shoulders. She looked so cute, like some kind of snow princess. He gazed downwards at her curved hips and shapely legs. He was getting frisky and could feel an erection start to push against his jeans, trying to point north. It was like a sexual compass, homing in on the one true direction. And he wanted to follow it and discover Katherine's nether regions. Christ, he was so horny. He wanted to take her then and there. But he couldn't. She was his client. He'd just have to calm down. Maybe have a roll around in the snow. "After you," he said, and gestured at the large front doorway.

Katherine skipped up the front steps, biting on a fingernail, feeling energised by the little flirt she'd just had with Richard. That is what it had been, wasn't it? He had flirted with her, and then checked her out. She was excited by the way his eyes had travelled up and down her body, mentally undressing her, and she was suddenly jolted by a pulse of pleasure between her legs.

Richard followed her up the steps, watching her bottom as she walked towards the door. Perfectly shaped and so inviting, he imagined pulling down her blue jeans to reveal what he guessed were the sexy, yet classy, panties beneath, barely covering her smooth, peach like butt. He longed to hold it in his hands, and then playfully stroke her, taking in the full curve of her buttocks, before encircling her trim waist and the sensual arch of her back. He dreamed of kissing the naturally golden skin of her shoulders, and twirling her hair between his fingers. Once he'd explored there, his hands would move purposefully to her front. What was waiting there was the nearest thing to heaven on this earth. He was suddenly jolted out of his fantasy by Katherine's voice calling his name. He'd been miles away, lost in the dreamscape of her body. God, he was going to have to get a grip on himself. If he didn't watch it, she was going to notice the large bulge in the front of his pants.

"Are you okay Richard?" said Katherine, stepping into the warmth of the hotel lobby and taking off her jacket "You looked like you were pre-occupied." She shook the snow from her hair and gestured for Richard to hand her his coat.

"I'm okay. Just thinking about the hotel. How it's going to look when it's finished." He deliberately kept his coat on. If he removed it, she'd see his hard-on for sure. She'd have to be blind not to see it. It was trapped in a southerly direction prevented from rising up by the seam of his jeans, and continued half way down his thigh. He busied his mind thinking about the designs for the hotel restaurant, hoping that would ease the tightness he felt in his crotch, and spare him the embarrassment of having to show Katherine around her hotel with an eight inch boner fighting its way out his pants.

Katherine stepped closer to Richard and brushed the snow from his coat shoulders. She started to undo the buttons one by one.

Richard was suddenly unsure of himself. Was she seducing him? He stood perfectly still, slightly startled. He felt his pulse quicken and his breathing became shallower. There was no way he was going to be able to resist this.

Katherine was toying with him. "There, that's better," she said, all the buttons now undone. "It's warm in here. You don't need this thing on." She stepped behind him and waited for him to surrender his coat.

He shrugged it from his shoulders and Katherine took it, hanging it next to hers. She glanced over at him and her eyes settled on the front of his jeans. She bit her lip to stop a little gasp of pleasure from leaving her mouth, her eyes widening, her pupils dilating. She took a deep breath to calm herself, her firm breasts rising and falling gently, silhouetted by the tight fitting top she was wearing. She was hard herself, and her nipples strained against the crisp cotton, threatening to pop the buttons on her blouse. She'd caught a brief glimpse it earlier, of course, as he'd walked up the steps. The outline of the beast that lay behind the zipper had taken her breath away, and she thought it funny how she could read Richard's mind by staring at his pants. Now she was just having a bit of fun. But she couldn't allow herself to fall for him.

Theirs was a business relationship. There was work to do. The hotel had to be finished. She kept trying to tell herself that as she led them both to the hotel lounge, Richard limping slightly behind her, clutching a briefcase close to his body, attempting to conceal his tumescence.

They emerged into the lounge and Katherine was pleased to see that there were logs burning in the fireplace, and a fire screen around it. She'd phoned ahead earlier and had asked the security guard to turn the central heating up, light the fire, and then leave them to talk business. He had a room at the back of the hotel and she guessed he'd made himself comfortable there, watching TV and eating potato chips. Somehow, the fire brought the hotel to life, and it made it much easier to concentrate on work if she wasn't shivering from the cold. Most weekdays the hotel was full of contractors putting the finishing touches to the rooms. That's why she'd asked Richard to meet her there at the weekend. They'd have the place to themselves. She thought about that decision, and realised that at the time she'd been innocently thinking about having enough peace and quiet for them to work. Now she wondered if they might be taking advantage of the privacy in other ways.

She picked up the iron poker and prodded one of the logs, levering and wedging the poker under it to allow air too circulate and get the fire roaring. She sat down on the nearest sofa and warmed her hands. She looked around. The place was really coming together well. The dream was nearing completion.

Richard sat down opposite her, nodded in approval at the progress that had been made since his last visit, and was relieved to see that the electricians had done a good job. The lighting was soft and low, not the temporary, harsh industrial light that had been cast over the room during the building stage. The gentle, atmospheric light would help conceal his erection, which was only now starting to calm down.

"Is all the electrical work complete?" he asked, trying to take his mind off of Katherine's body, and get down to work.

"Yeah. It's all done. Wiring, lighting, security system, you name it. Everything's done. On schedule as well. We might actually be able to make up a bit of the time we've lost. We'll hopefully be open by Easter."

"Great. So, it's just the restaurant, the kitchens and the big bedroom suites to do."

"Kitchen's in already. It was completed last week."

"Wow. I can't wait to see it," said Richard. "I don't suppose there's any food there? I'm kinda hungry after the drive up from Denver."

"I usually keep a few things to snack on when I'm here in the week. We'll find something you like."

Richard knew what he wanted to eat. But he wasn't sure if he'd be dipping his fingers in Katherine's honey jar. He'd have to settle for donuts and coffee. "Just some cookies will do. Something to take the edge off my appetite."

Katherine was inclined not to give him anything, wanting to keep him hungry. She wanted him to be ravenous. If he was getting his mouth around anything today, she damn well hoped it would be her. "Let's take a look," she said, and led the way to the kitchen.

The two of them strolled through the maze of rooms, their minds on each other, both wondering when, or if, one of them would make the first move. Lost in their thoughts, they didn't notice the discreet hotel security cameras tracking their every move.

Chapter Two

There wasn't much food in the kitchen, but enough for Katherine to rustle up some pancakes and coffee. Before pouring the batter into the skillet, she dipped her middle finger into the bowl and tasted some. Her pout ran along the length of her finger, engulfing it, and licking it clean.

Pancakes and coffee. Richard felt it was like the morning after the night before. Only without the night before. At least not yet. Even the way she prepared food was sensual. Her movements were fluid and graceful, and he watched as she flipped the pancake over. He'd really been looking forward to seeing her again. It had been too long. His heavy work schedule, flying all over the world, left him little time for serious relationships, and although he'd been seeing a girl in California, it had eventually come to nothing. The first time he'd met Katherine it had been instant attraction. Lust, for sure. But also something deeper. Now, here in the hotel he'd designed for her, watching her fix him some food, he felt strangely content. It felt good.

Katherine placed the pancakes on a plate and put them on the table in front of Richard. "Maple Syrup?" she asked, hovering the bottle over his plate.

"Yeah. Sure," replied Richard, and he watched it flow all over the perfectly round pancakes. He took a mouthful, enjoying the sweetness and the silky smooth feel of the syrup.

Katherine sat next to him and cut a piece of pancake with the edge of her fork, swirled it around in the syrup before delicately putting it into her mouth. She ran her tongue along her lips, licking every drop.

Richard felt himself getting frisky again, and he shifted in his chair to get comfortable. His leg brushed against Katherine's and he felt the warmth of her thigh against his. To his delight, she didn't move it away and they sat eating their pancakes, excited at their physical connection.

They finished, and Katherine cleared the plates from the table. She ran some water into the sink and searched for something to clean them with. She suddenly felt Richard's presence behind her, and her heart skipped a beat. She turned around and he was standing next to her. She knew what he wanted. She wanted it as well. She had thought she'd make him work for it.

Keep him on edge. But all those thoughts had disappeared, and she wanted to have him immediately.

Richard tried to say something, but she put her finger on his lips and shook her head, brushing her palm lightly along his jawline, her eyes never leaving his.

He couldn't hold back any longer, and he pulled her towards him, their lips thrust together in a sensual soft collision. He loved the feel and taste of her, and was intoxicated by the sweet smell of her skin. He ran his hands along her curves until they rested on her hips. He felt her perfect bottom through her jeans, driving him crazy with desire. His hands returned to her front, and he started to undo the buttons on her blouse.

Their lips disconnected, and Katherine's breathing became quicker and shallower as she watched him unbutton her. Her hands moved down to his jeans, and she unfastened them nimbly. She slipped her hand inside his shorts and felt his pulsing cock. He was rock hard, and she ran her palm down the length of his shaft and gently squeezed his balls. He groaned in pleasure. She felt a sense of urgency, an aching to have him inside her. Any foreplay could wait until later. Afterplay. Right now, she just needed to be taken hard and fast. She needed release from months of pent-up frustration.

Richard removed Katherine's blouse and unhooked her bra, revealing her breasts. He pulled her against him, kissing her neck and shoulders and slowly tracing a line with his lips downwards until he reached one of her now erect nipples. He ran his tongue over it and bit gently, sucking, and caressing it playfully.

Katherine gasped, and ran her hand through his hair. But she was impatient for more, and gently guided his hand towards her jeans, gesturing that he remove them.

Richard had been hesitant earlier in the evening, but he now moved with more purpose. He unbuttoned her jeans and slid them down, caressing her thighs as he did so. The silkiness of her skin was almost too much to bear, and he imagined parting her beautiful legs, and lying between them as she wrapped them tightly around him. He stepped back briefly and removed his own jeans. She sat up on the kitchen worktop as he removed her remaining clothes, everything except her panties. Richard pulled off his shirt and then, starting at her ankle, he ran his tongue up the inside of her leg until he reached the gates of heaven. He kissed her panties and started to peel them off of her.

Katherine lifted her bottom, allowing him to more easily remove her lingerie, and she giggled as he slid them down the length of her legs, over her feet, and nonchalantly threw them to one side. She clamped her legs around his torso and put her arms around his neck, inviting him to lift her on to him.

His penis quivered as it strained ever upward, searching for the warm haven of her vagina, desperate to bury itself in her. To feel the silky warmth of her holding him tight. To become one with her. Richard lifted her up, their naked bodies joyfully connected, their lips exploring the contours of each other's body. Their senses heightened, enjoying the feel, taste and smell of each other.

Richard put her down gently, yet purposefully, on the kitchen table, where she lay with her legs apart, her pussy wet and welcoming, ready to receive him. Sensing her urgency, he climbed on top of her and let her hand guide his penis towards her. The head of his cock brushed against her soft and beautiful vulva, knocking at the door, but not yet entering. He knocked again, and this time her pussy lips yielded to the forward thrust of his cock.

She moaned as he entered her, and she ran her hands down his torso to his butt, pulling him deeper into her. Needing him to fill her. She wanted him to envelop her. To feel she was surrounded by him, his weight pinning her to the table, unable to escape. To have him possess her.

Richard began to move rhythmically, at a pace that was pleasurable but not so fast that it would be over too quickly. He wanted this to last for as long as possible. To savour every second. Every moment inside her was bliss. The sweet caress of her pussy was wonderful. Her vulva was beautiful. Luscious labia, like silk veils, concealing the pink palace beyond. The palace in which he could quite happily spend the rest of his life.

Katherine could feel herself building to a climax, a warm fire glowing within, and an impatience for it to burn brighter and consume her completely. She ran her hands up and down Richard's back, settling on his shoulders for a moment, before frantically moving back down to his buttocks, pulling him inwards again, dictating the pace, desperate to take his full length.

Their bodies moved as one. Like beautifully oiled machines, they worked in tandem to bring each other to the point of no return. Muscles relaxed and contracted fluidly, hearts beat in perfect rhythm, their breathing as one. Katherine squeezed her legs tighter around him, heightening the pleasure of each stroke he took in and out of her. She was almost there. She could stand it no longer. Another second or two and she'd come. It was overwhelming. The warmth started to spread from between her legs and engulf her entire body. Her toes curled in pleasure as her muscles tensed. Just one more stoke. That's all she needed.

Richard, felt the contraction in her muscles and knew the moment had arrived. He was longing for release himself, and he gave one last powerful thrust into her, filling her with his cock.

Katherine screamed in ecstasy as she came, and the powerful orgasm washed over her. Every nerve-ending in her body tingling in delight. Her desire satiated. Her body satisfied. Her soul uplifted.

Richard came as he felt her vagina tighten around his cock. He relaxed and allowed the pleasure to release itself from his body. He exhaled as the fluid coursed rapidly from his balls, up his cock, and flowed into Katherine. He slumped against her, wrapping his arms around her, stroking and kissing her.

They lay still for a while, holding each other close, letting their heartbeats return to normal. It was Katherine who spoke first. "Well. That was kind of unexpected."

"What? My performance?"

"No," giggled Katherine. "Just that it happened at all. I thought we were up here to do work this weekend."

Richard nodded. "This is better though. Huh?"

"Much better," said Katherine, and she snuggled closer to him.

TJ Squires didn't know whether to feel turned on, or just angry. He sat in the chair in his room at the rear of the hotel. A microwave burger in one hand, and the other one massaging his cock through his pants. His eyes were glued on the video monitor in front of him. Not quite believing what he was seeing, but getting angrier by the minute. How dare that architect sonofabitch do that to his woman. She might not strictly be his. But he'd had his eyes on the lady boss since the security company had sent him on the job a few weeks ago. And, boy, was he aching for her. Any woman, in fact. Six years in state prison would have that effect on a man.

He'd been released three weeks ago after serving time for taking part in an armed robbery. He hadn't actually been carrying a gun, but he'd roughed up the staff at the store pretty badly. It wasn't his first crime. There had been other robberies. Mostly small time. Bars, shops, a jewellery company. And other, more serious, crimes too. Sexual assaults. Not that he'd ever been caught. If he'd done time for all his crimes and misdemeanours he'd be doing life. No, he'd been lucky over the years. It was only that last job that had gone wrong. If there hadn't been a couple of cops in the store, stocking up on donuts, they'd have got away with it.

He was given early release for good behaviour. Who'd have thought it? TJ Squires and good behaviour weren't exactly words you'd usually hear together in the same sentence. It had been six long years without a woman. And he was ready to make up for that now.

Upon release, a friend from inside had fixed him up with some false paperwork, and he found himself a job with a security company. So much for their vetting process. They made a big play with clients about how their guards had been fully checked out. Bullshit. A short form to fill in, the briefest of interviews, and the job was his. Pathetically easy.

What he hadn't counted on, however, was that he'd be sent to guard some hotel construction high in the Rockies. He thought he'd be around town, close to the bars and the women. Instead, he found himself cooped up most of the time in the back room of an unfinished hotel, with only contractors for company. It wasn't so different from prison. But then, one day, she'd walked in. He noticed her first on one of his monitors. She was like one of the Playmates from the magazines he'd had in his cell. He'd been dreaming about a woman like her for so long. And the moment he saw her, he vowed he'd have her.

He hadn't been too concerned when he heard that the Boss would be meeting the hotel's architect at the weekend. He thought it would be strictly business, and was even looking forward to it. He didn't usually get to see her at the weekend, and if she was around the hotel, all the more chance to check out her tits and ass. Maybe, he'd even spot his opportunity to get it on with her - the architect leaving early, her staying behind to do a bit more work, him doing his rounds, a chance to be helpful, a quick chat, some flirtation. And then, she'd be his. How could she resist him? Years of working out in the prison gym had given him a hell of a body. She'd fall for him straightaway. He had it all worked out. Only, he hadn't counted on her and the architect doing that.

When the boss and the architect had started making out in the kitchen, he'd felt that familiar anger rise up inside of him. The anger that the correctional facility psychiatrist had correctly pinpointed as the source of all his troubles. The anger he'd been told he had to learn to control. But how could he, when things like this happened? Some jerk of an architect messing with his woman. It wasn't right. It couldn't be. He was going to have to teach them both a lesson. No-one fucked with TJ Squires.

Chapter Three

Katherine opened the door to the spa area and went in, closely followed by Richard. They placed their clothes on a bench, and she fiddled with a control unit to get the steam room working. "Should be ready in about twenty minutes or so."

"Great. I love a steam bath."

"Me too. Especially in cold weather," said Katherine, picking up a bottle of shower wash. "Let's take a shower first."

"Sounds good," replied Richard.

They walked into the large, marble tiled shower, turned it on, and shut the smoked glass door behind them. A jet of cold water powered downwards, but very quickly reached a comfortable temperature.

Katherine blissed herself out under the hot water, splashing it on to her face with both hands, and letting it run through her hair.

"Are we the first to use the showers?" asked Richard

"We're the first *couple* to use them," said Katherine. "But I did try one of them out a few days ago. Why? You're wondering if they're working properly?"

"No. It wasn't that. It looks like the've done a great job," said Richard. "I was thinking we might find some way of christening them."

"What did you have in mind?" said Katherine, running her hand over Richard's chest.

"I thought that maybe a little bit of lovin' in the shower might be a good thing. You know, create a kind of positive vibe for the spa."

Katherine laughed. "I've heard some lines before, from guys who wanted to get inside my panties. But, having sex in order to set a positive vibe for the hotel is definitely a new one. Very original though. I'll give you that."

"It's true," protested Richard, "Uh…in the classical world they used to believe that if a couple made love in a particular place, the surroundings would somehow absorb those feelings, and then make the place lucky."

"Is that true?"

" Yeah, for sure," said Richard. "Don't you believe me?"

"Sounds like it could be true," said Katherine, "I guess we better test the theory."

"Always good to test these things," replied Richard, nodding his head.

Katherine squeezed some shower gel on to her palm, worked up a lather with her hands, and started to wash Richard, admiring his physique as she did so. His tan covered almost his entire body, except for a white hoop of skin around his middle where his shorts had been. "You didn't sunbathe naked, then?"

"Not quite. They don't allow that type of thing in Dubai?"

"They're kind of strict, huh?" said Katherine. "What would happen if they caught the two of us making out in a hotel spa?"

"Jail, probably."

"I wouldn't mind being trapped with you in a cell for a few days."

"More like a few years. And it would definitely be separate cells."

"I guess we'd better enjoy our five American freedoms here and now, then"

"Five freedoms?"

"You know. Freedom of speech, freedom of worship…"

"Don't you mean the *four* freedoms?"

"Uh-uh. Five. Speech, worship, freedom from want, freedom from fear…"

"And?"

"And. Freedom to make love with whoever you want, wherever you want, whenever you both want it."

"I must admit, it's a new one on me."

"I guess you'd better get to know it, then. By getting in plenty of practice."

"Practice makes perfect."

"Exactly."

"Exactly," repeated Richard, and pulled Katherine towards him, loving the feel of her wet body against his. He took some of the gel and started to massage her breasts. They were full and perky, and he enjoyed gently bouncing them up and down, cupping them in his palms. He lowered his head and took her right nipple into his mouth, flicking it with his tongue, thrilled at the way it grew harder in his mouth. He became aware of Katherine's hand on his shoulder, pushing him downwards, indicating she'd like his mouth to get to work lower down her. Understanding her request, he slid his hands along her curves until they rested on her hips, and lowered himself on to his knees, finding himself face to face with her neat little strip of hair. He buried his face in her, his hands on her butt, pulling her towards him.

Katherine placed one hand on the marble wall of the shower, and adjusted her stance, opening her legs wider. An invite for Richard to explore her more deeply.

Richard manoeuvred his head between her legs, the warm shower washing over them both, relaxing their bodies, bringing suppleness to their limbs. He flicked his tongue upwards and along the delicate opening of her vulva. Her labia now engorged and moist with the natural juices that were springing forth from inside her. His fingers massaged her outer lips, and prised them further apart. His tongue continued to explore her, enjoying the taste and aroma of her, and the feel of the juicy flesh which he now held firmly in his mouth, pulling and kissing gently, patiently opening her up. Her labia now apart, he pushed his tongue upwards and into the candy pinkness of her vagina.

Katherine moaned and began to move her hips rhythmically, sliding her vulva across Richard's mouth, eager to have his tongue taste her and penetrate deeper. The hood of her clitoris had now receded, and her pleasure button glistened moist, proud, and now desperate, itself, to feel the touch of his mouth.

Richard explored the inside of her treasure chest, but remained aware of the pearl that lay just outside, amongst the divine and beautiful folds of her vulva. It, too, needed to be shined and polished and loved with the same care and attention to detail that his tongue had shown her other jewels. It was just that he was enjoying her succulence so much that he wanted to drink his fill before leaving. She could wait a moment more. The longing would double the pleasure when the gift was finally received, and the anticipation was sweet for the both of them.

Katherine's movements were becoming more erratic. Her smooth undulating rhythm was now interspersed with more intense shudders as Richard's tongue moved in and out of her pussy, and along the length of her vulva. Several times, it had brushed fleetingly over her clitoris, teasing her, seducing her with the promise of transcendence, before withdrawing. As if to whisper to her, *if you're a good girl, you too can experience nirvana.* And she was a good girl, wasn't she? Didn't she deserve it? If not, what else did she have to do? But it wasn't up to her. It was Richard's move. And if he was the man she thought he was. A good man. Unselfish. Then, they would glide into paradise together.

As if sensing Katherine's thoughts and needs, Richard withdrew his tongue from her honeypot, but instead of making for her clit, he rose up from the tiled floor and in a singular fluid motion grabbed the shower head with one hand, and gently steered Katherine downwards and on to all fours with the other.

Katherine's mind was in a frenzy. What was he doing? She certainly hadn't seen this coming. Her heart raced in an adrenaline rush. Her clitoris crying out for release.

Richard adjusted the shower head to its vibrate function and placed it between her legs, firing straight at her clit. His aim was spot-on. A sharp shooter of the shower world. He hit Katherine right on the bullseye. Only it wasn't him who'd get a prize, it was Katherine. The rhythmic pulsing of the shower sent wave after wave of pleasure through her clit and she quickly reached the moment of launch. Any second now and she's be through the stratosphere. She mentally counted down, and got from ten to four in just two seconds.

Richard had his free arm around her stomach and he could feel the contractions of her muscles. She was close. Real close. He continued the countdown she had started. "THREE…"

The sensations were now almost unbearable.

"TWO…"

Katherine let out involuntary squeals of delight. It was becoming too much.

"ONE…"

Her entire body convulsed in ecstasy. Her mind exploded blissfully, and she tugged at Richard, pulling him on to the shower floor, where she threw herself against him, demanding their flesh be together, insistent that he hold her close.

Richard started laughing. "I guess that was LIFT OFF, huh?"

Katherine mumbled a yes.

Richard kissed her head and pulled the shower closer, letting the warm water flow over their bodies, gently soothing them both.

It was a few minutes before Katherine said anything. "So you are a good man after all, Mr Ford"

"Not completely good," replied Richard. "I've got a little confession to make."

Katherine raised her head and looked at him.

"That thing I said about the Greeks and Romans believing that making love somewhere would bring good luck. Well, it wasn't strictly true."

"You mean you made it up?"

"Something like that."

"It was a lie?"

"Just a little one."

Katherine laughed. "How can I ever forgive you?"

"Well. You can look at it this way," said Richard. "Lies are quite creative, really. They require imagination…"

"And..?"

"And. If I wasn't such a creative soul, I wouldn't have thought of using that shower head on you. And right now, who knows, you might still be on the launchpad at Planet Frustration."

"You have a point."

"Not that I needed the shower head, of course. I've got a highly skilled tongue."

"I noticed."

"Maybe, I'll show you again later. Show you what magic it can perform."

"Promises. Promises," said Katherine.

TJ Squires was madder then hell. He'd been in the spa room for the last ten minutes, his eyes never leaving the glass door to the shower. Beyond it he could see the shadow play that Katherine and the architect were putting on for him. If they thought he would enjoy it, then yes, they were half right. Despite himself, he couldn't help but get hard at the thought of Katherine's soapy flesh, all glistening skin, and ripe breasts and butt. But they were also wrong. Dead wrong. They were mocking him. People had mocked him before. And they'd paid the price.

He rooted around amongst their clothes on the bench, and pulled out Katherine's panties, placing them quickly in the pocket of his uniform. He'd enjoy those later.

He looked around, unsure of what to do next. He could just rush into the shower and confront them. The architect would be so shocked, he'd have no chance. A few slaps around the face, a knee to the groin, and then slam his head into the marble wall. It might not kill him, but it would incapacitate him for the foreseeable future. He could always tie him up and leave him outside in the snow. He wouldn't be found for months.

TJ Squires cursed the fact that he didn't have a gun. He'd been hired for the less responsible job of *guard*, not security *officer.* The hotel had insisted on that. It was so out of the way, and unfinished, that they didn't feel they needed an armed guard. If anything had happened, a robbery, a shooting, or, God forbid, a death, it would have got the hotel off to a bad start, creating not just bad karma, but one hell of a lot of negative publicity. No-one wanted to stay at a hotel with blood on the carpet.

It was all for the best for TJ anyway. If he'd been armed, it would have meant extra security checks and a license. Something he was unlikely ever to get with his criminal record. He'd just have to rely on old fashioned brute physical force, and his rat-like cunning.

He listened to the sounds of pleasure from inside the shower, and the internal red mist engulfed him again. After the first incident in the kitchen, the architect may have just gotten away with the beating of his life. But now! Defiling his woman again, for a second time. That was a capital offence. He couldn't see how he could avoid killing him. The architect was making him do it. Belittling him. Taking from him the thing that was rightfully his.

Anyway, it was no big deal. He'd killed before. The last time, just two years ago, when he was in prison. That fag who had tried to touch him. No-one did that to TJ Squires. He'd been clever, though. Made it look like a suicide. Found hanging in the prison kitchen storeroom. Nobody had suspected TJ. After all, he was known for his good behaviour. Kept his nose clean, always respectful to the guards, put in a hard days work in the kitchen and the laundry. Read his bible every night. A reformed character, that's what the parole board said. What idiots. It was too easy.

He might be a fancy architect. With his degrees and his diplomas. From some Ivy League college, most probably. But it wouldn't mean sweet FA when he was dead. In fact it would be kind of ironic given what TJ now had in mind for him, and for the first time today his grimace broke into a broad grin.

The main hotel structure was built, but the contractors had only just broken ground on a small annexe to the side of the hotel. Somewhere to put all of the ski equipment. How ironic it would be if the architect were to end up in the foundations of his own hotel, buried under ten feet of concrete. For an architect, that was an act truly beyond the call of duty. And once he was entombed down there, TJ would have the lady boss all to himself. All his, to do what he wanted with. He'd take her every way he could, and then have done with her. The bitch had disrespected him too. She'd have to pay for that, no matter how cute she was. Maybe she'd be joining the architect in the ground. Both of them holding up there lousy hotel.

His excitement at his new plan managed to keep his anger under control, and he slipped quietly out of the spa room. He had something he needed to find.

Chapter Four

Katherine and Richard picked up some towels and walked with their arms around each other towards the steam room. It had reached its optimum temperature, and was perfect for relaxing tired limbs and unknotting tense muscles. It had two tiers of seating around its walls, the upper for those who could take the heat, the lower, slightly cooler. Richard clambered on to the top tier, his feet on the bench below. Katherine sat on the lower level, making a nest for herself between his legs, her arms resting on his thighs.

"Don't like it too hot, huh?" said Richard.

"Just taking it slowly," replied Katherine. "Besides, I think I'm at exactly the right height." And she leaned her head backwards, feeling Richard's cock against the back of her neck.

He ran his hands through her hair, scraping it backwards and twisting it into a loose, wet ponytail, before coiling it gently around his cock. He leaned forward and kissed her on the clear skin of her forehead, massaging her shoulders and stroking her upper body.

Katherine gave a deep sigh of contentment, her mind wandering, daydreaming, trying to make sense of everything that had happened today. Making plans for the future. Her future. Perhaps *their* future. Their future. That sounded good. "Richard…" she said.

"Yeah."

"Can I ask you something?"

"Fire away."

"Did you always like me? I mean, for the last two years, since I first approached you about the hotel?"

Richard found it surprisingly easy to answer. He usually got tongue-tied when talking about the emotional stuff, but now it seemed natural. "From the moment I first saw you."

"Really? Why didn't you say anything?"

"It was complicated. I was in a relationship already. With this girl I met in Hawaii. It was fun whilst it lasted, but I guess I always knew it wasn't really heading anywhere."

"Why?"

"I was busy with work. My practice had just started to really take off. She was more of a beach babe. She wanted me to just do a bit of freelance work, and for the both of us to go and live up on the North Shore."

Katherine laughed. "She wanted you to become a surfer dude?"

"Yeah. Something like that," said Richard, shrugging his shoulders. "Anyway. It wasn't really in my life plan. She was a free spirit. I was ambitious. She liked the sea. I liked the mountains…"

"You were too different?"

"Yeah. Way too different. The opposite of me and you."

"How do you mean?"

"When I first met you. The day you came to my office in Tahoe. I knew I'd met a kindred spirit. We both loved the same things. Architecture's my passion. And it's in your blood too.""

You wanted me because I like buildings? Doesn't sound so romantic," said Katherine.

"You know what I mean. When we discussed the plans for the hotel. The way your eyes used to light up. The way we talked about it until late into the night. It was wonderful. Maybe it's not romantic, but it's one of the things that made me fall in love with you."

Katherine tensed at the sound of the L word. "You love me?" she said, her voice betraying her emotion.

"Yes. Always have."

Katherine turned around to face Richard, her hair uncoiling itself from his erect penis. Katherine glanced at it and then kissed him deeply. "I love you," she whispered as their lips parted. It had only been thirty minutes since she had orgasmed. But she wanted him again. Only this time it was different. In the kitchen and the shower it had been lust, fun, who knows what, and for all she knew when they left the hotel later, it may be the last time they'd see each other. His work on the hotel was more or less over. Any remaining issues could be fixed over the phone, or be handled by one of his assistants. But now, everything was different. That one short L word had changed the game entirely.

She stroked his face and looked down at his cock, finding the urge to ride him irresistible. But before taking him inside of her pussy, she'd take him into her mouth. She bent down, grabbed his cock, and ran her tongue along it, enjoying its fresh-out-of-the-shower feel and taste.

Richard took a deep breath, and leaned back against the wall. The steam seemed to create a dreamlike atmosphere, edges were blurred, sounds were muffled, and movements slowed. Watching Katherine go down on his cock seemed like something from a fantasy, other worldly, like gazing at life through a veil, making it all the more beautiful, as it forced his imagination to complete the picture, and softened any imperfections. Not that Katherine had any. It was only the physical sensations that made it real. So real. Her touch was exquisite, and he wasn't sure if he could stand the pleasure much longer, as her tongue danced on the head of his cock.

Katherine pulled back his foreskin and took him fully into her mouth, using her hand to slide him in and out, her warm tongue teasing him, her lips kissing him. She hoped he'd stay the distance, wanting to climb on to him as soon as possible. She grabbed his balls firmly, before loosening her grip and stroking them with her palm. She looked at his face. He was in another world, his eyes closed, a dumb grin on his face. He was enjoying it. Of course he was.

Richard could feel himself about to come, and he clenched his muscles, trying to delay the inevitable. Holding out a bit longer. He laughed out loud. The pleasure was driving him crazy.

Katherine took him out of her mouth, kneeled in front of him, and placed his cock between her breasts, pushing them inwards with her palms, ensuring the fit was snug and tight. She began to move them up and down, stroking his cock with them.

Richard responded with a a series of rhythmic movements, his penis sliding up and down through the beautiful little tunnel Katherine had made between her breasts. Her skin was lubricated with steam, and his foreskin retracted and advanced with each forward thrust and withdrawal, heightening his pleasure.

Their foreplay was wonderful, a few pleasurable opening acts, but not the main event. She watched Richard glide between her tits. "Which do you prefer?", she asked him.

"Huh?" said Richard, only half understanding what she said. He was too far gone for speech. His other senses were so overwhelmed that talking seemed an almost impossible thing to do.

"Mouth, tits or pussy?" said Katherine "Which?"

Richard groaned. "All three. All three at the same time would be good."

"You'll have to grow another two to do that."

"OK…they're all great… but I really, really want your pussy."

"You sure?"

"Yeah. I've gotta have your pussy. "

"Right now?"

"Right now. Immediately…seriously, I'm not gonna hold out much longer. Now. Please, please, please, please."

"Okay," said Katherine, hopping to her feet, and sitting astride Richard's legs, lowering herself on to his waiting cock.

He entered her with ease. Her syrupy pussy, parting to allow his full length to slide effortlessly into her, until he could go no further, his balls tight up against her. He placed his hands on her butt, taking some of her weight, and aiding her up and down movements. He kissed her breasts, moving quickly from one nipple to the other, not wanting to ignore either. He brought one of his hands round to her front so it was caught between them both, and worked his fingers down towards her clitoris, where they began to stroke her.

Katherine placed her hands on his shoulders, allowing herself to move harder and faster. Her hair fell down onto his head, and she closed her eyes, hypnotised by the intense rhythm she had now worked up to. Her breasts jigged around Richard's face, her nipples straining towards his mouth. She was nearly done. She came down heavily on him again, feeling her pussy slap against his balls. A few more of those and she'd be there. Up and down again, their loins grinding against one another, her clit swollen almost to bursting point. This was it. One more stroke from Richard, and it'd all be over. A primal moan rose in her throat, and with her remaining strength she lifted herself once more and slammed her pussy back down to meet Richard's upward thrust. She gasped and writhed in pleasure as his cock buried itself deep inside her. Her entire body buzzed with an electrical energy, as the intense orgasm spread throughout her limbs.

Richard grabbed her tight towards him, buried his head in her breasts and pushed his cum into her. Eager for her to receive his gift, wanting to mix his juice with hers. Thoughts of contraception had never even crossed his mind tonight. Who cared? If she did get pregnant, then great. He'd marry and start a family with this woman tomorrow. Today, if he could. She had to be his. And now she was.

Richard sat back against the wall and Katherine slumped against him, exhausted and satisfied. They lay there for a few minutes, holding each other close, letting their breathing return to normal, their bodies aching pleasurably. Their minds in awe of the wonderful thing that had just happened. Aware, that their lives might not be the same again.

They eventually arose from the post-sexual slumber they'd fallen into, and left the warmth of the steam room. Richard grabbed a large towel and wrapped it around Katherine as she dried her hair with another. She glanced over at the large mirror on the wall above the vanity area and looked at herself. Her golden complexion now flushed pink from the heat and the orgasm. She watched Richard in the mirror, as he dried himself, pulled on a T-shirt, and wrapped a towel around his waist. She ran some water into the basin and the vapour rose and clouded the mirror. Richard's image slowly blurred. She splashed water onto her face and looked at herself again. Suddenly, she let out a scream. The steamed up mirror had revealed a message written on it. She stepped backwards, her hand covering her mouth, reading it over again to make sure she wasn't imagining it. She wasn't. It was still there: FUCK U. TONITE U FUCKIN DIE.

TJ Squires rooted frantically through all of the equipment in the storeroom. Where was it? He knew it was here somewhere. He'd signed for all this shit when it had been delivered last week. He just couldn't think straight. It was always like this. The anger took over, and he couldn't calm down until it was done.

He took another mouthful of whisky from the bottle he was carrying, and wiped his mouth with the back of his hand. He threw aside some chairs destined for the dining room, kicked some fire extinguishers over, and then finally found what he was looking for. A delivery from the catering suppliers. A full set of top quality Japanese chef's knives. He ripped open the package and sorted through the various types. He held them in his hands, weighing them up. They were good. They'd do nicely. But which one?

The carving knife was good. Long, slim, elegant, ultra sharp. This would gut the architect real well. Slice him open like a pig at the slaughterhouse. But it didn't feel right.

TJ looked around some more until his eyes finally rested on the meat cleaver. Now that was his type of weapon. He could swing it down on the architect and damn near cut his head off. He ran the cutting edge along his forearm and it drew blood instantly. Perfect.

He went back to his room, and with a swipe of his arm cleared the desktop, sending everything crashing to the floor. He threw the cleaver into the desk, embedding it's blade deep in the oak top. He yanked the liquor bottle from his pocket, taking another swig, and then rooted deeper in his pocket and pulled out the panties he'd taken. She wouldn't be needing these. Make it all the easier for him to get into her.

He put them down on the desktop, smoothing them down with his hand and stroking them. It was a long time since he'd seen something like these. All those years working in the prison laundry, washing the disgusting worn clothes of his fellow prisoners. It had been a humiliation. And it was time someone paid for all the crap he'd had to put up with.

He drank some more whisky, and threw the empty bottle at the wall. It shattered, sending glass shards around the room. He opened the desk drawer and pulled out another one. Brandy, this time. Easy Jesus. He took a sip, wincing slightly. He held the bottle over the lady boss's panties and let a few shots worth drizzle over them, fascinated as the liquor soaked into the silk. He picked them up and put them into his mouth, slurping the liquor from them. Sucking Easy Jesus from his woman's panties. That was the nearest TJ Squires was ever going to get to heaven.

Fortified by the drink, he pulled the cleaver from the desktop and left his office, slamming the door closed behind him. The time had come. Payback time.

Chapter Five

Richard put his arms around Katherine. "Don't worry, honey. It's probably been there a while."

"I didn't see it before."

"It's all the steam from the shower, the steam room, the basin. It just didn't show up before."

"You think so?"

"Yeah. It'll be the contractors, just messing around."

"You're probably right."

"Don't worry. You've got the security guards here haven't you?"

"Yes. One of them, at least."

"Okay then. We'll go and see him. Ask him to have a look around the place. Make sure there's nothing wrong."

Katherine nodded, put her blouse on and looked through the jumble of clothes. "Must have left my panties in the kitchen."

"We better go and pick them up before the security guard does. He's going to wonder what's been going on."

Katherine relaxed, and slung a towel around her neck. "We wouldn't want him knowing about that, would we?"

"We'll get them on the way back to the lounge," said Richard. "Besides. I like the idea of you not wearing any."

They wandered barefoot to the kitchen and had a quick look around, but still couldn't find them.

"They'll show up somewhere," said Richard.

"Yeah. On eBay probably," replied Katherine, a nagging voice in her head telling her to keep looking.

"Let's look again later. We better get some of that work finished."

"Okay. But let's go and see the guard first."

"Do you know him?"

"Seen him around. But haven't really spoken to him, much. He's from an agency," replied Katherine. "I think he's called TJ."

"Where's his office?"

"He's in a temporary room at the back. We put all the monitors and stuff in there for now, until the other room's finished."

They made their way to the guard's room and knocked on the door before entering. Immediately, they were hit by the smell of hard liquor and stale sweat.

"It's a bit ripe in here," said Richard.

Katherine nodded. The room was in a mess. And she felt herself getting angry that the security guard was treating her hotel like a pigpen. And where was he, anyway? Doing his rounds? Or sleeping off his hangover somewhere?

She made her way over to his desk to leave a note, when suddenly she saw them. Her panties. She picked them up. They were wet, and she tentatively held them closer to her nose. They stank of liquor, and she looked at the bottle of brandy next to them.

Behind her, Richard let out a scream, and she spun around, her heart suddenly racing. Richard was hopping around on one foot, and trying to pull something out of his other one with his fingers.

"What is it?"

"I stood on some fucking glass," he said, removing a two-inch shard from his heel, his foot and hand covered in blood. He hopped to the nearest chair and sat down.

Katherine rushed over to him and examined the wound. It looked worse than it was. She made sure the glass was removed, took the towel from around her neck, and wrapped it around Richard's foot. "That'll do for now. There's some first-aid equipment in the kitchen."

"Where the hell's the guard?" asked Richard.

"I don't know," replied Katherine. " But I've got an uneasy feeling about this. My panties are on the desk over there."

"What?"

"Somebody put my panties on the desktop. And they're soaked with brandy."

"Brandy?"

"Yeah. There's something wrong here. I think we should leave. Get back to town."

"You think?"

"It's for the best," said Katherine. "Maybe it's something and nothing. But this, and the mirror. I don't know!"

"The weather's pretty bad outside. We could always put in a call to the sheriff's office. You know him, don't you?"

"He's an old family friend," said Katherine, searching for the phone. "He's been sheriff of Steamy Springs for years." The phone was upside down on the floor by the side of the desk. She picked it up and dialled. Nothing. She tried again. Still nothing. There was no dialling tone. The connection was dead.

Richard got up from the chair and followed the phone cable to the wall. It was plugged in. "Looks okay. Maybe it's the snowstorm. He peered out of small window. It was dark, but he could see that it was still snowing heavily.

"Do you have your cell?" asked Katherine.

"I left it with my work stuff, in the lounge. Yours?"

"Same."

"Right. Let's go and try the cells. If we still can't get hold of anyone, we'll try and get back to town. Sound okay?"

"Yeah. Sounds good."

"We'll have to take your SUV. I don't think my Porsche is going to make it in this weather."

"We should be okay. I've got snow tyres," said Katherine. "Even if we can't get to the town, we can make it to the the next hotel down. *The Mountain Inn*'s only about a half mile away."

"Okay," said Richard, taking hold of Katherine's hand, leading them to the lounge.

As they left the guard's office, Katherine glanced at the video monitors. "Oh my God!"

"What is it?"

She pointed towards the screen "One of the cameras is focused right on the kitchen table."

"Shit," said Richard, "He saw everything."

They ran into the lounge and went straight over to the sofa, looking for their cellphones. They were missing. "I'm sure it was just here, on top of these papers," said Katherine

"Mine as well," said Richard.

"Maybe we can…" She stopped in mid sentence as the lights went out, and the double doors of the lounge slammed shut.

"Looking for these, are you?" said a voice from by the door,

They could see somebody standing in the semi-darkness about twenty feet away. His body barely visible in the firelight, his face obscured by shadow. He was holding something up for them to see.

"Who are you?" said Richard.

"Shut the fuck up, builder-boy."

"Is that you, TJ?" said Katherine, standing close to Richard.

"You know its me, sugar. Who'd you think it was?"

"What are you doing, TJ?"

"I've come to claim what's mine."

"Put the light back on and give me the cell," said Richard.

"I don't think so," said TJ Squires, throwing the phones into the corner of the room. "I may not have your college education, but don't take me for some stupid fucker. Got that?"

He moved closer to them, and they could finally see him.

"What the fuck are you up to?" said Richard, in two minds as whether to try and hit the guy.

"Richard. No," shouted Katherine, spotting the glint of metal in one of his hands. "He's got something. A knife."

TJ Squires held up the large cleaver and swiped it through the air, backwards and forwards. Making a hissing sound through his teeth. He laughed. "Still feeling brave, builder-boy?"

Richard backed away at the sight of the cleaver. It would take his hand off if he tried to wrestle it from him.

"Why are you doing this, TJ?" said Katherine, trying to reason with him.

"You should know, honey."

"I don't know what you're talking about."

"Think."

"I have no idea."

"You just fucked this asshole. Not just once. Three times," shouted TJ Squires. "You fucking betrayed me."

"What?"

"You belong to me, bitch."

"You're deranged," said Richard. "She barely knows your name."

"She'll know me soon enough."

"Don't do anything stupid, TJ," said Richard, trying to calm him down.

"Fuck you," said TJ Squires, and he lunged at Richard with the cleaver.

Katherine screamed as Richard dived to one side and on to the floor, narrowly avoiding the blade hacking into his arm. Katherine backed away behind the sofa, trembling.

Richard tried to get to his feet, but wasn't quick enough. TJ Squires was looming over him with the cleaver. Richard edged backwards along the floor, trying to escape this madman.

TJ Squires looked at the bloody towel around Richard's foot and kicked it. "Not the only blood you're gonna spill tonight."

"For fuck's sake. Why are you doing this?" shouted Richard.

"Didn't I make myself clear?" said TJ Squires. "You messed with my woman. And now I'm gonna remove the offending piece of your body."

Richard's eyes filled with fear, and a cold sweat formed on his brow.

"That's right, builder-boy. Maybe I'll slice it off," said TJ Squires, running his finger along the cleaver's blade. "Then I'll fry it on the fire there, and she's gonna fucking swallow it whole, since she likes the fucking taste of it so much." He pointed the cleaver at Katherine.

Katherine held herself tight, trying to control her trembling

Richard managed to scramble to his feet, but was now backed into a corner. He picked up a chair and held it in front of him. TJ Squires took a swipe at the chair, and cut one of the wooden legs clean off. The cleaver was razor sharp. If it could do that to wood, bone and flesh was not going to be a problem. Richard couldn't see a way out. Desperately, he threw the chair at TJ, but he deflected it away with just a shrug of his powerful shoulders.

TJ Squires had the architect cornered like a hunted fox. Now he was going to rip him apart, before burying him in the foundations.

Richard was defenceless. Whatever he did, he'd get some part of himself sliced open. There was no hiding from the cleaver.

TJ Squires took one final look at Richard's eyes, wanting to see the fear.

He lifted the cleaver high in the air, preparing to swing it down on Richard's head. He pivoted his torso so as to put the maximum amount of force into his blow, and his arm began its downward swipe. He then let out a dreadful scream.

Katherine smashed the red-hot iron poker into the side of TJ Squires' head. The force of the blow knocked him sideways, and his swipe at Richard missed, embedding the cleaver deep in his own thigh. There was a cracking of bone and sinew, and blood spurted out and around the room. TJ Squires squealed like a wounded animal.

Katherine hit him a second time. Straight in the face. The heat of the poker searing his flesh, the strength of the strike, cracking his face open. TJ Squires slumped backwards and crashed to the floor. He was out cold.

Richard and Katherine didn't want to wait around and see if he was dead or not. They picked up their cell phones, found the car keys, and bolted for the door. They jumped into the SUV, Richard driving, Katherine making a call to the Sheriff's office.

The snow was still heavy, but the SUV handled well. Richard was used to driving in the mountains in winter. Ten minutes later they were at *The Mountain Inn*, relieved to see the place alive with people. They were welcomed by the staff, who Katherine knew, and were ushered quickly into a private lounge.

Twenty minutes later one of the Sheriff's Deputies arrived to talk to them, explaining that another four officers, including the Sheriff himself, had gone up to *The Spa in the Clouds*.

They sat together on a sofa, both feeling lucky to be alive. Richard put his arm around her and she put her head on his chest. All they could do now was wait.

Chapter Six

TJ Squires lay on the bed in his cell at the State Penitentiary. After attempted murder, assault with a deadly weapon , and violation of his parole, he wouldn't be going anywhere, anytime soon.

He didn't remember much about the night he was arrested at the hotel. He'd woken up hours later in a cell at the county jail, with his thigh bandaged up, a broken nose and cheekbones, five missing teeth, a ten inch diagonal burn across his face, and the mother of all headaches. He was still getting the headaches now.

He was probably looking at twenty years, every day of it on twenty-three hour lockdown. He cursed that bitch of a boss and her asshole boyfriend, and he vowed that one day he'd get his revenge.

"I declare The Spa in the Clouds officially open," said Katherine Chase, cutting the ribbon in front of her. The assembled guests clapped and cheered, eager to look around the new hotel.

Robert Chase put his arm around Katherine. "Well done, Kate. I always knew you'd pull it off."

"Thanks Daddy. Do you like it?"

"It's great. A fantastic addition to the family empire."

"I hope it will be," said Katherine. "Me and Richard are really going to try and make this the place to be."

"Don't go putting my other hotels out of business," said Robert, laughing.

"Wouldn't dream of it," said Richard. "And talking of other properties, I hear you're planning building some luxury lodges on the other side of town."

"Could be."

"Need an architect?"

"You offering?"

"Well, I'm gonna be around here quite a bit from now on," said Richard. "I'll need something to keep me busy."

" You're moving your office from Tahoe?"

"That's the plan," said Richard, looking at Katherine. "Now that I've got a reason for staying in Steamy Springs."

"Let's talk about it next week," said Robert Chase, seeing an old friend over the other side of the room "You two enjoy your party. The real hard work starts tomorrow."

Katherine locked arms with Richard. "Well, we did it. Finally."

"*You* did it," said Richard. "It was your project."

"Couldn't have done it without you, though."

"We make a good team, huh?"

"Yeah, I think we make a pretty good team," said Katherine. "And not just at work, either."

Unlawful Entry

Chapter One

Jessica Chase left the small boutique clutching a bag containing her purchase, and made her way back to her Jeep. As she was crossing the road she heard a voice call out to her.

"Hey Jessica. You been buying something to surprise me with?" said a man, leaning out of the window of a Chevy Tahoe.

Jessica turned quickly to see who it was, her long blonde hair swishing through the air and falling around her shoulders. Her eyes settled on the Chevy and its driver, sunglasses covering his eyes. Who was it? She wasn't sure.

He lifted up the dark shades and smiled. "Recognize me now?"

"Caleb?"

He nodded.

Jessica hurried over to to the SUV, slightly bemused that she was feeling excited to see him. "Caleb. Is that you? I haven't seen you in…what…two years?"

"Been a while, Jess," he said. "Too long."

"What are you doing? Did you leave the Sheriff's Department?" she said, gesturing at the blue Chevy he was driving.

"No. Still there."

"You on your day off?"

"No. I'm working right now."

"Last time I saw you , you were driving a black and white."

"Yeah," said Caleb. "That was back when I was on Patrol. I just made Detective. About three months ago."

"Congratulations," said Jessica. "So. Are you on a stakeout or something?"

"Nah, I was just passing, when I saw you go in the store."

"You don't miss much. Guess that's why you made Detective so quickly," said Jessica, looking back at the lingerie boutique she had just come out of.

Caleb laughed. "You know all the residents know each other's business in Steamy Springs."

"You're right. Sometimes I think I should stay in LA."

"Can't keep away though, huh?"

"Guess it's in the blood."

"Well, your family do own just about everything in the town."

"Not everything," replied Jessica. "Just some of it."

"Most of it."

"Okay. Most of it," said Jessica, letting the shopping bag twirl around her suntanned legs.

Caleb nodded. "You must have finished college by now. You coming back home? Or staying out in California?"

"I don't know. Haven't made up my mind yet. I'm just back for the summer," she said. " Maybe I'll stay. Depends."

"Depends on what?"

"You've sure become nosy since you made Detective," said Jessica. "You weren't this chatty with me when we were at high school. Or when you were *Patrol Officer* Blake."

"Yeah. It's difficult to switch off," said Caleb. "This job's all about asking questions."

Jessica looked at his bare forearm resting on the window frame, shirt sleeves rolled to the elbow. He looked like he was still in good shape. And tanned. "So what assignment are you on at the moment then? Apart from watching women entering and leaving lingerie stores. The Sheriff's department widened it's remit has it?"

"You know we're interested in anything and everything that goes on," said Caleb, "You never know. There could be a theft from that store some day. I've gotta know my patch."

"I can assure you, I didn't steal this," said Jessica, one hand on her hip, and her other outstretched arm holding the bag, the handles resting on her upturned palm.

"I believe you," said Caleb. "But I might have to examine the contents of the bag."

"I don't think so, Detective Blake," said Jessica, trying to sound offended, but finding it hard to suppress a laugh. "Some things are private."

"Caleb nodded. "Lucky guy."

"Who?"

"You know what I mean."

"Women do buy these thing for themselves, you know. It's not just for the benefit of some guy."

"Whatever."

"Whatever?"

"Yeah. Whatever you say," said Caleb. "But I've been past that shop plenty of times. I've seen the kind of stuff they've got in the windows. Exotic. Who knows what else they've got inside. Maybe the Sheriff's Department could source their handcuffs from there."

"It's not *that* kind of store. Just sexy lingerie and clothes That type of thing. Cute stuff."

"Cute stuff! As I said, lucky guy."

"Okay. I think we better end this conversation here and now," said Jessica, glancing at her watch. "I've got an appointment."

"That's too bad. Maybe we can continue this some other time."

"Yeah. Maybe." said Jessica "I'm free for most of the holidays."

"Okay. I'll work something out." Said Caleb, grimacing slightly. "I'm a bit busy with work at the moment, especially with the Economic Forum on. There was another break-in last night."

"Where?"

"Some banker's lodge. On the edge of town. Must be worth millions."

"Same as last year, huh?"

"Yep," said Caleb, straightening his tie. "With all the big shots in town this week, the Sheriff's cancelled virtually all leave.

"You on the case?"

"Uh-huh. I guess it's my chance to show the Sheriff he made the right decision making me Detective."

Jessica nodded. "Any leads?"

"Not as yet. We're keeping an open mind on whether last years burglaries are related to last night's"

"Could be the same guy. It was during the Forum last year as well, wasn't it."

"Yeah. When all the rich Wall Street types are here."

"And their wives, with their million dollar jewellery."

"Rich pickings."

"I remember daddy talking about it last year. He was worried it might damage the tourist trade in town."

"The Sheriff's going to be meeting with your father later. Tell him to beef up the security at his hotels."

"He's out of town at the moment. But I heard a whole load of delegates checked in at the *Rocky Mountain Lodge* yesterday," said Jessica. "My sister's new hotel's got a few VIPs staying too."

"*The Spa in the Clouds*?"

"Yeah. They've only been open three months. Last thing they need is any trouble."

"Especially, after that crazy security guard with the meat cleaver they had there," said Caleb, stroking the light stubble on his face. "Your sister sure gave him a beating with that fire poker. Don't mess with the Chase women, huh?"

"That's right," said Jessica. "We can look after ourselves if we have to."

"I never doubted it," said Caleb, looking Jessica up and down. She really was a beautiful girl. He'd been in love with her since their school days. Every guy had. He was a year older than her, and one thing or another had always stopped him asking her out on a date. If he was honest, he'd been a little intimidated by her. By all the Chase girls, in fact. They were the four most stunning sisters you were ever likely to meet. And their old man was the multi-millionaire who damn near owned most of the resort. Steamy Springs should have been named Chaseville. The family had built the town from nothing. And now it was up there competing with Aspen for the swishest resort in the Rockies title. For all their money, though, they were a down-to-earth family. There'd been no private education for the girls. Old man Chase still drove around in an old Ford. They didn't demand any special treatment. Respected the independence of the Sheriff's Department. But, they were super-rich, nevertheless. Most folks were intimidated by that kind of money. The Chase's could definitely look after themselves. Caleb just wished that one day he'd get the chance to look after Jessica. Also, no other girl could fire him up the way she could. Just the sway of her hips or a fleeting glance from her blue eyes was enough to do it. She was walking viagra. A steroid shot to his cock. She was so hot, she should be on prescription. Caleb's mind was now miles away, dreaming about removing that pretty little summer dress she had on.

"You OK?"

"Yeah. I was just thinking about work," said Caleb, shaking himself out of his daydream. "We're under real pressure to catch this guy."

"Is he dangerous? Anyone get hurt?"

"Doesn't seem to be. He usually waits until everyone's out. But who knows, maybe he's carrying. Why? You worried?"

"Not really."

"You're at home alone at the moment, then?"

"Just for a week."

"Where are your folks?"

"They always get out of town when the Economic Forum's on. I don't think my father likes all those bankers and politicos too much."

Caleb nodded as he took in the information. "You want me to stop by?"

"I guess you could do," said Jessica. "For a little while."

"I'm working late tonight, but maybe I'll call round before I get off duty. Okay?"

"Sounds good. See you later then."

"Looking forward to it," said Caleb, as he started the engine and nodded goodbye.

Jessica realised that she had enjoyed her little flirt with Caleb. It was fun. Sometimes the guys at her college could be a little too earnest. Flirtation seemed to be a problem for them. Unless they'd had a gallon of liquor beforehand, and then flirtation just turned into a kind of drunken rambling. Not their fault though, they were the generation who'd been indoctrinated with political correctness. A lot of the fun had been taken out of life. The sexual dance between men and women was as old as time, and something natural and joyous. Pity there were too many humorless creeps around, trying to remove all the *joie de vivre* from people's lives. Caleb was a bit different. Small town guy. Kind of old fashioned in some ways. A little rough around the edges, but with a good heart. Good looking. Sexy. Definitely sexy. Maybe she wouldn't mind him getting his hands on her lingerie after all. It was a pity she hadn't just bought some new pieces.

She hurried back to her car, and mentally went over her plans for the evening . She felt both excited and nervous at the same time. Caleb was a good guy, and she hated herself for what she was about to do. But, nevertheless, it had to be done.

Chapter 2

The sun was setting over Steamy Springs. Night had come. Jessica pulled the curtains across the windows of her large bedroom suite, and removed her robe. Light from the adjoining bathroom bounced off her golden skin as she bent down to take the item from the shopping bag.

She sat on the edge of her bed, naked apart from a pair of sheer, seamless french knickers. She put her long, lithe legs into the new garment and then slowly pulled it upwards over the rest of her body. She fastened the zipper. The black catsuit fitted perfectly, accentuating every curve of her body. Her hips nicely rounded, her breasts full and firm and held securely by the tightness of the suit. She then wiggled her toes into black climbing shoes, and tied the laces.

She'd had to buy the new catsuit because her old one had ripped the night before, whilst climbing down from the upstairs window of the banker's lodge. Growing up in these mountains, climbing was second nature to her. She'd been doing it all her life. Cat burglary, however, was something she'd only gotten into in the last few years. Nothing beat the thrill. And, it was all in a good cause.

Jessica tied up her hair, put on some thin gloves, and put a rolled up ski mask on her head. She'd pull it over her face later. She slung a black pack across her shoulder and headed for the door.

The Chase's lodge was on the slopes above the town, surrounded by trees, and not visible from the road. The house she was about to break into was only about five minutes away on foot. She could make it without being seen fairly easily, but getting in there was going to be tougher.

Tonight's victim was Charles Szabo, a Wall Street financier who seemed to be behind just about every big corporate takeover of the last few years. Especially if they were hostile. He had a reputation as a ruthless operator, and it was usually bad news for the workforce if he took control of the company. He was just the sort of person Jessica despised. He got rich from destruction, not creativity.

She slipped out of the house and, in her black outfit, seemed to disappear into the dark night. She quickly reached Szabo's palatial lodge. Twelve bedrooms, fourteen bathrooms, two indoor pools, and only occupied for about ten days a year. She knew the layout well. Her Father's company had built it, and it had been easy for her to get access to the architect's plans. She'd been in it once before. After it was completed, but before it was sold.

Despite the size of the house, she knew that Szabo liked to live simply when he was in town. He didn't have permanent staff, and used the cleaners and security people from one of the resorts many service companies. He also came without his wife or any other family members.

Jessica pulled down her ski mask, covering her face, climbed over the perimeter wall and jumped down into the garden. It was a thirty second sprint across open lawn to the house. Jessica hesitated. There were probably motion sensors, and security lighting, at the very least. She didn't want to risk having to deal with anything like that. She edged across the side of the grass lawn, keeping in the shadows provided by the tall trees.

Her eyes scanned the house for any signs of life. There were a few lights on downstairs and some of the upstairs windows were bright. Then she found what she was looking for. What every burglar prays for. An open window on the first floor with a curtain fluttering from it in the warm evening breeze. And a convenient balcony she could climb up to. It was too good an opportunity to miss, and she doubted that any other part of the house would provide a better access point. She crept within spitting distance of the house and dived the last few feet, crouching on the floor, waiting for an alarm to ring out or a floodlight to illuminate the grounds. Nothing. This was going to be easier than she thought.

The lodge walls were built of local stone and had a rough, rustic quality to them. Ideal for climbing up. Jessica reached up the wall with her hand and found a stone to grip on to. She tried a few places with her foot and eventually found a spot which she could stand on. Little by little she scaled the wall until she reached the balcony. She pulled herself up and on to it, and quickly stood flat against the wall at the side of the balcony door. She peered into the room beyond. It was bathed in a gentle light from a floor lamp, and, to her relief, there was no-one there.

Jessica's mind raced, assessing the situation. Was there anyone in the house? There were a few lights on and the balcony door had been left open, but the house seemed quiet. The Economic Forum had a big gala dinner going on at one of the hotels tonight. All the big shots would be there. She was guessing that Szabo would be there too. And, anyway, she hadn't come this far to back out now. The risk was part of the thrill of doing it. It was now or never.

She took a deep breath, steadied her nerves, and slipped quickly inside. She moved over to the bedroom door and out onto the landing. She paused for a minute to listen for a sound, and to let her eyes get used to the gloom.

Her night vision now improving, she glided through the first floor of the house, her feet barely making a sound on the thickly carpeted floors. She knew where she was heading. To the master bedroom. It had a dressing room off of it, and she guessed that if there was any jewellery in the house it would quite likely be in a safe or strongbox in one of the closets. If there was nothing there, she'd have to head downstairs and find Szabo's study.

It was a huge, rambling house with many wings, and hidden corridors. The master bedroom took up the entire west wing of the first floor, and Jessica quickly located it, her memory of the house serving her well. She put her hand on to the door handle and was about to ease it open, when she suddenly stopped. There were voices. Someone was inside.

"Shit," she murmured to herself. Her heart stepped up a gear and she clamped her mouth shut, muffling the sound of her breathing. She inhaled through her nose and calmed herself. Panicking now would get her caught. You needed ice cold nerves in this job.

There was nothing for it, she was going to have to retrace her steps. Maybe get back out on the balcony. Wait for whoever it was to leave, and then try again. She wasn't going to give up so easily. She guessed it was Szabo in there. And if anyone deserved to have some of his valuables stolen it was him. Talk about ill gotten gains. She may be a thief, but not as big a crook as Szabo. He'd pocketed billions over the years from insider trading and manipulating stock prices for his own end. His takeovers had led to the loss of tens of thousand of jobs. The deals were always sold as being good for the company. They were only ever good for Szabo.

She put her ear against the door and listened again. She heard some music and then some voices. It was a TV show. Someone was watching television.

Or maybe, they'd just forgotten to turn it off. She was in two minds as what to do. She'd come this far. It was worth taking a risk.

She pushed the heavy wooden door very slightly and peered into the room. There was a small bedside light on, but the room was mainly illuminated by the glare from the TV set. There was nobody in the bed, and the entrance to the dressing room and bathroom beyond looked dark.

She pushed the door further and went inside. She quickly took in the layout of the room. The bed was unmade, with a quilt half on the floor. But, other than that, it was tidy and looked almost unlived in.

Hurrying into to the dressing room, she turned on the light and worked her way through the closets. Most were empty. Two at the end, near the bathroom had clothes in. Suits. Shirts, Ties. Nothing much casual. She opened the final closet and stood back in amazement. It was packed full of the most hardcore gear she'd ever seen. Black leather straps, knee length lace up boots, masks, bullwhips, chains, sex toys, something hanging up that she could only describe as a gimp suit. Shit, he could open a store with this stuff. She rooted around a little, pulled out some DVDs and looked at the covers. Lots of half naked men in black leather who looked to be doing weird things to each other. Jessica could hardly suppress a giggle as she looked at them. So Szabo liked men did he? No wonder he never brought his wife here, or have any live-in staff. Gave him plenty of time and space to indulge his tastes. Don't suppose Mrs Szabo would be too happy to find out about this. Or maybe she knew already. Maybe she joined in somehow.

Jessica put back the DVDs in the same place, and closed the door. It had been an interesting and unexpected discovery, but she still hadn't found what she was searching for. She'd been sure there would be a safe somewhere in the closets. But nothing.

She rolled back the sleeve of her suit, and looked at her watch. She still had time to check downstairs. But she needed to get back for when Caleb arrived. If she managed to find any valuables tonight, or if Szabo somehow realised that someone had been in the house, at least she'd have some sort of alibi in Caleb.

She made her way downstairs, not bothering to sneak, now confident that there was nobody at home. She checked through the maze of rooms until she came to what looked like a library. She wasn't going to risk putting on the ceiling light so she took a small torch from her rucksack, ready to use when she needed it.

A six drawer walnut desk was at the end of the room. Jessica looked through them one by one. Lots of paperwork. A diary. Keys. Personal organiser. Some pens. An old cell phone. Nothing exciting. She stood up and checked the painting on the wall behind the desk. A portrait of Szabo himself. What an ego that guy had. She pulled the bottom edge of the frame away from the wall and checked to see if there was anything behind. Nothing. Szabo must have a safe or strong room in the house someplace. But where was it?

It was then Jessica noticed that a section of the fitted bookshelves that lined the walls of the room appeared to be at an odd angle. She knew straightaway what it was. A concealed doorway, and Szabo had been very careless to leave it slightly open. Perhaps he'd left in a hurry. Or, maybe he was in there.

She pulled the shelving section outwards and it opened smoothly. She shone the torch inside. There was a short corridor and some steps leading down at the end of it. She walked in.

At the bottom of the steps was a large metal door. She'd found it. He must have had the cellar converted into a strong room. She tried the handle on the door. It was locked.

There was no way she could bash it down. This was the real deal. He's obviously gone to a lot of expense to make sure no-one could get in there without the key. And there was a digital combination lock on it. That wasn't necessarily a problem. She had a little gadget in her backpack that could deal with that. It would just take a bit of time. She checked her watch again. She's be cutting it real fine if she did it now. It was too much of a risk. If she came back tomorrow night or later in the week, she'd have more time. Szabo was around all week. He was giving talks at various events during the Forum week. He was delivering the keynote speech at some party on Thursday. And, she'd discovered, he'd be giving a press conference on Friday. Jeez, that guy was so full of himself.

Reluctantly she went back up the stairs and closed the bookshelf doorway.

She took a deep breath, collected her thoughts and decided she would leave it till later in the week. Right now, she just had to get back for Caleb.

Jessica left the house the way she had got in, and hanging from the balcony, she let herself drop the last few feet to the ground. Within a minute she was back over the wall and heading home. As she traversed the hillside back to her house, she could see a vehicle winding it's way up the narrow road towards the Chase property front gates. It was Caleb in his SUV. She'd have to be quick. He'd be buzzing the intercom any moment. She sprinted to the house, fumbled with the back door lock and let herself in. Kicking off her climbing shoes, she pushed them with her bare foot into a closet and threw her rucksack and ski mask in too. No time to change out of the catsuit, though. She looked at the mirror in the front hallway, let her hair down and wiped a slight sweat off her brow with her sleeve.

The intercom sounded. She looked at the video screen. She answered, slightly breathless. "Hi Caleb. I'll just open the gates. Come on up."

"Sure thing," replied Caleb. "You okay?"

"Yeah. Why?"

"You sounded a bit out of breath."

"Just finished a workout."

'Okay. See you in a second."

There was a knock at the front door. Jessica answered, and she gestured for him to come in.

He looked her up and down and his face lit up in a big, toothy smile. "Nice outfit. That what you bought at the store today."

"Could be."

"Put it on just for me, did you?"

"I was working out in it."

"Interesting choice of exercise wear. Looks real tight. What are you training for? A pole dancing career?"

"Very funny," she replied, hand on hip. "And, yes, it is tight."

"In all the right places, I see."

"Thank you. You been working out as well?"

He ran his palm over his hair and checked it for moisture. " I just took a quick shower when I got off duty."

"Do that for me, did you?"

"Never know when you'll get lucky. Best to be prepared."

Jessica felt a sudden urge to kiss him. She wasn't sure why. She hadn't really expected anything to happen tonight. But the thrill of her little escapade to Szabo's lodge, her feeling kind of sexy in her catsuit, and, she guessed, just the fact that Caleb had cared enough to come over after a long shift to make sure she was okay. She couldn't help but love him for that. Plus he looked pretty hot. And she'd always loved that smile of his. He was the one lawman she might be willing to give up her cat burglary career for. What the hell. She liked to live dangerously. "You just gonna stand there and admire me from a distance, or you gonna to help me get out of this thing?"

Caleb needed no further encouragement. He stepped towards her, his hands reaching towards her hips. "That's what we law enforcement officers do, you know."

"What?"

"Help women out of tight situations."

"Chivalry isn't dead, *Sir* Caleb."

"Wait till you see my lance," he said, as he pulled her towards him.

Chapter 3

Charles Szabo let the applause of the audience wash all over him. He loved the limelight, and never more than when it was an audience of his peers. The biggest names in world finance, as well as senators and congressmen, Fortune 500 CEOs, and foreign leaders. They were all here tonight to listen to what he had to say about the world economy. He'd been bullish, of course. He always was. He'd told them exactly what they wanted to hear. More deregulation. Freeing up the banks. Letting them do whatever they wanted to do. No holds barred, buccaneering, free market capitalism. He loved talking about money, and they'd loved it when he announced the details of his latest deal. He couldn't wait until his keynote address on Thursday. Even the President would be there.

Once the cheers and the clapping had died down, he went back to his seat, and knocked back a glass of whiskey. He glanced at his Rolex. He'd have to suffer the dinner for the next hour or so. But then he'd leave. Once off stage, he usually didn't care to stay too long. It didn't interest him to listen to anyone else's speech. Why would he? He had the answers. The more thoughtful politicians and economists, with their talk of more regulation and increased taxes for the rich, were idiots. What the hell did they know? He's once joked with a Senator that he'd be more than happy to pay double what he was paying in tax right now. And as he was currently paying no tax at all, double a zero, and you'd still get a big fat zero. Taxes were for the little people.

The success of the speech and all the talk of money had made him horny as hell. It was time he left. Feeling agitated, he got up and headed for the door. The car valet would have his Bentley ready outside. He needed to get back home to the lodge, go down to the cellar, and see to those two men he'd got chained up in his own private dungeon.

Chapter Four

Caleb carried Jessica up the stairs to the bedroom, put her down on the bed, and lay by the side of her. He traced a long line of kisses along her jawline before meeting her lips. Their soft moistness feeling good against his. His hand glided along the curves of her body, over her hip, and on to her rounded bottom, which he pulled closer, wanting to feel her warmth against him.

Jessica undid the buttons on his shirt, one by one, until his chest was exposed. She ran her fingers through his chest hair, tugging it slightly, before turning her attention to his nipples. She let her fingers brush lightly over them, feeling them spring to life, before tweaking them harder between her thumb and forefinger, watching Caleb's face for clues as to whether he enjoyed it.

He did. And he needed to explore Jessica's body as she was exploring his. He located the zipper on the catsuit, pulling it downwards, and urgently removed her from it's tight grip. Once the close fitting fabric had been peeled back from her upper body, he saw that she was almost naked underneath. Her golden skin glistening, her breasts full and firm, her nipples erect, eager for his touch. He removed the rest of the catsuit, and she lifted her bottom off the bed to allow him to slide it downwards, grabbing her panties as well when he saw the first glimpse of them. He wanted no more barriers between them. She lay naked on the bed, and Caleb shrugged off his shirt and kicked off his jeans and boxers, revealing his nakedness to her for the first time.

Jessica looked at his large, swollen cock and, as if due to some primitive reflex, grabbed it with her hand, squeezing it tightly, before releasing the pressure, only to tighten it again a second later. She let go of it, and ran her open palm along its length, her fingers feeling the contours of his balls, wanting to know every inch of him. She wriggled lower in the bed and pulled his cock towards her mouth. Her lips brushing against its head, her tongue moistening its tip. She licked along its length until she reached his large balls, which she then took into her mouth, gently and delicately, as if eating two chestnuts, still hot from the fire. She moved them around in her mouth, letting her tongue caress them, and her lips massage them, enjoying the taste of her man.

Caleb lay back on the bed, one hand on Jessica's shoulder, the other on the top of her head, twirling her hair between his fingers, and pushing her head back down when she appeared to be loosening her mouth's grip on his balls. Jeez, he was loving this. There was something about having your balls sucked that was so pleasurable, but also, at the same time, there was a tinge of fear mixed in with it. They were such a sensitive part of a man's anatomy that some almost primitive fear of having them bitten off was never far from his mind. He had to have complete trust in his partner, and he looked down at Jessica and knew that she only wanted to pleasure him, and would not harm him.

Jessica let his balls from her mouth, and said goodbye to them with a passionate kiss. She looked at him with a cheeky grin on her face, as if to say *wasn't I a good girl doing that for you, and, yes, I enjoyed it as much as you.* She crawled back up the bed, and lay down on him, chest to chest, stroking his unshaven jaw and kissing him deeply.

Caleb tasted something unfamiliar on her tongue that hadn't been there earlier. It was the taste of his own body on her, and the thought of their intimacy only heightened his own arousal, and made him all the more eager to taste her. He swapped their positions, and flipped her over on to her back, before diving in to her body, wanting to devour her. He traced his tongue down her stomach until it reached her navel, where he probed his tongue in and out, before sucking her into his mouth, the taught skin of her stomach barely yielding to the vacuum created by his lips. It was just a tease, alerting her to what was about to come. Letting her know that his mouth would very soon move on to the more fleshy and moist delights of her vulva. And where, unlike her belly button, his tongue could extend inwards and taste the sweet honey juice of her pussy.

Jessica guided his head downwards, desperate to have him between her legs, longing to feel the warmth of his mouth against her. She moaned as he finally reached his destination, and his tongue began to play amongst the slickness and folds of her vulva. She grabbed the bed sheet and clenched her fist tightly as she felt Caleb fleetingly lick her clit, before he moved on again to continue to kiss and suck her now engorged labia.

Caleb pushed his head deeper into the warmth between her legs, his senses intoxicated, but not yet overwhelmed, loving the taste, feel and fragrance of her pussy, burrowing instinctively, knowing that more than anything else in the world he wanted to be here right now, with her, and inside her. Her pussy was now very wet and his tongue slid easily inside. He began to rhythmically thrust and withdraw his tongue, and with each inward movement, took as much of her as he could in his mouth.

Jessica let the ripples of pleasure wash over her body, a foretaste of the larger waves that would soon engulf her. She tugged at Caleb's shoulder wanting him to move further up her body and, in doing so, allow his cock to replace his tongue inside of her.

He was reluctant for his mouth to leave her pussy, but at the same time, his cock ached to be held tightly by her. He got to his knees and pushed her legs up and apart. He looked briefly at her beautiful pussy, its lips apart revealing the luscious pinkness beneath. His cock quivered as it sought out her pussy, and its head brushed against her vulva and over her clit.

Jessica pulled Caleb's body towards her, wrapping her legs tightly around him, not wanting to let him go. She needed him now. She needed him hard and deep within her. She wanted to feel their bodies become one.

Caleb's cock found its way through the double gates of her labia, and glided effortlessly into the moist tight tunnel below. A perfect fit. He began to move in and out, the pleasure heightened by every forward thrust, as her vaginal walls gripped him. He lowered his upper body onto her. And felt her swollen nipples against his chest, and the firm full breasts below. His lips found hers and their tongues played together in the warm caves of their mouths.

Jessica, now pinned to the bed by Caleb, ran her hands along his back, drawing invisible contour lines with her fingers as she silently mapped every square inch of him, taking in all the valleys and peaks of his muscles, claiming the territory as her own.

Their bodies worked together effortlessly, like experienced dance partners who moved instinctively, muscle-memory rendering thought unnecessary, knowing each others minds, anticipating the next turn or pass.

Caleb began to move quicker as he felt Jessica's grip on his shoulders tighten, her fingernails beginning to dig into his flesh. His own breathing became more rapid as if trying to imitate hers.

Jessica was nearly there. Each thrust from Caleb was sending electrical currents through her. The grinding of his pubic bone against hers stimulating her clitoris and making the pleasure almost unbearable. She clamped her legs more closely around him, tightening her pussy around his cock. She moved her hands down onto his firm butt and controlled his movements, pulling him ever deeper and harder into her. She felt his cock extend right into her, as deep as it could go, his balls slamming against her vulva. She pushed him out again before, almost aggressively, drawing him back. The pleasure was nearing it's climax. Her mind began to swirl, and her conscious thought melted away, as she let the intense feelings take her over. Nothing else mattered now, she wanted him to be inside her, and waited for the ecstasy of release. She was there. Caleb came down and into her one last time, and the tidal wave she longed for finally crashed down on to her and carried her away helplessly. She cried out as the nerve ending over her entire body pulsed with pleasure, and her pussy released it's warm juices to intermingle with Caleb's.

Caleb felt himself come inside her, and he buried his head in her neck, as his weary body slumped against hers. He felt her warm breath on his shoulder and heard the moans of pleasure from the same open lips. Her body was wonderful. Firm yet soft, and inviting, and perfect. He ran his hands through her long hair and gently kissed her. He felt overwhelmed with this woman. The way he had never really felt with anyone else. A curious mixture of uncontrollable lust mixed with intense feelings of warmth, affection and protectiveness towards her. Was this love? Was this the woman for him? The *one*?

They lay together for a while, their bodies slowly regaining strength, finding joy in each other's embrace. Post sexual bliss at its best. No worries. No regrets. Just warmth and happiness, and the relief that they had finally found each other.

Caleb kissed her and held her close, and she snuggled against him. He pulled the comforter over them both, and they dozed merrily, not wanting to leave the warmth of each other or the bed.

Jessica put her leg over his and played with his cock. "Well, that was good."

"It was, wasn't it," said Caleb. "Finally."

"What do you mean, finally?"

"Been waiting a long time to be with you."

"How long?"

"Probably since the first time I saw you. When we were teenagers."

"Really?"

"Yeah."

"You didn't say anything."

"Guess I figured if it was going to happen, it was going to happen. And tonight it did."

Jessica nodded. "Worth the wait?"

"Oh yeah. Definitely worth the wait. Big time."

She smiled, put her head on his chest and closed her eyes. She felt overawed by her feeling towards him, but didn't know if she could let this happen. She thought she'd had everything planned for this summer. She knew exactly which houses she was going to target, she knew which people deserved to lose a little bit of their wealth, after they'd taken so much illegally or immorally from others. It had all seemed so right and so easy when she and her friends discussed these things at college. She was sure the Occupy movement were basically correct in what they were doing, but she now wondered if the methods her own little cabal had decided on were the correct ones. The one thing she hadn't planned on was falling in love with Caleb. And now there was a conflict between her social ideals and her heart. She didn't want to hurt Caleb, or get him into trouble. And as he lay beneath her, drifting off to sleep, she pondered what to do next. Heart or head? It was a dilemma as old as time itself.

Chapter 5

Caleb woke first, an organic alarm clock in his brain telling him it was time to get up and go to work. Jessica was still lying on him, fast asleep.

He moved her gently as he tried to get out of bed, but she stirred and held on, not wanting him to go. "Stay a bit longer."

Caleb didn't really need any extra encouragement. He'd woken up with a huge hard-on, which had only got firmer still when he'd pulled back the comforter and caught the early morning light shimmering on Jessica's naked body. She looked beautiful. That, together with the softness of her skin against his, was making him as horny as hell, and like all men, he loved sex in the morning. There was no finer way to start the day.

He put his arms around her and pulled her close, his warm cock nestled snugly against her butt, his hands gently massaging her breasts, his lips kissing her shoulders, and nuzzling the back of her neck.

Jessica giggled as she felt the heat of his cock. "You feeling frisky?"

"Uh-huh."

"Me too. A little."

"Just a little?"

"I'm a bit sleepy."

"It'll wake you up," said Caleb, laughing. "Better than coffee."

"I bet it will. Just wake me up slowly, though."

"You want it in a kind of laid back style, huh?"

"I like getting laid in any style. But in the mornings I like nice, easy, comfortable sex."

"You want me to do all the work?"

"Maybe not all of it, but that would be nice, honey."

"I'll see what I can do," said Caleb, amused at Jessica's candour. He placed his hand under her top leg and lifted it higher, exposing her pussy. He let her leg rest on his and he slid his finger tips between her labia, opening her up, making sure he could enter her easily. His fingers sank into her and he pushed her moisture upwards, before withdrawing them and finger painting her pussy juice onto her clitoris, which was now emerging from its hiding place, eager for his touch.

Jessica lay with her face on the pillow and closed her eyes, as if the loss of sight might heighten her other senses and make the pleasure more intense. She felt for Caleb's leg and squeezed his thigh, An unspoken command for him to continue.

He flicked his cock against her butt cheeks a few times as he manoeuvred it towards her vagina, rubbing its head along her opening, lubricating it with her honey juice. He entered her smoothly and slowly until his penis had travelled its full length, and began to glide in and out of her. He placed his hand on top of hers, interlaced their fingers, and guided them both down between her legs, where they stroked her clit together. He let her hand dictate the pace so that he might better understand her body's needs, and adjust his own rhythmic movement in time with her. He kind of liked this slow pace as well. There was no sense of urgency. He would come in good time, and it would be all the better for the slow build up to climax.

Jessica lifted her head from the pillow and craned her neck sideways, her lips searching for his. She kissed him softly, and rubbed her face against his, before letting her head fall back on the bed. The morning sleepiness was now leaving her body, and with it the need for a more lively pace took over her thoughts. She scrambled up onto her hands and knees, making sure that Caleb moved with her, not wanting his cock to leave her. She spread her legs wider, inviting him to take her harder and faster.

Caleb kneeled behind her, pushing deep in to her fully exposed pussy. His hands gripped her hips, and he pulled her on to his cock, his eyes taking in the beautiful curve of her butt as it seemed to slam down onto him with each thrust.

Jessica placed her hands on the rail at the top of the bed, clenching it tightly, her head slumped down between her outstretched arms, her long hair falling on to the bed. This was bliss. Being fucked by her man in the first light of morning. She moved her butt in a circular motion, in time with Caleb's own movement, and the rhythm was replicated by her breasts which swung freely beneath her.

Caleb moved up real tight against her, his thighs almost holding her. He slid his palms up her back and gripped her shoulders to steady her as he began to pump faster and faster. He wasn't going to hold out much longer. So much for slow sex. He needed it fast now. Hard and fast. And he upped his stroke rate as if racing for a finish line.

Jessica, too, was having second thoughts about her easy, comfortable sex thing. This was good too. Real good. And she gave in to the moment, and embraced the change of pace. She wanted him harder than ever, and she was glad that he had taken her from behind, allowing him to let rip and completely bliss her out with each deep penetration.

They both came together, as he gave a final, powerful thrust. His cock buried deep, his body slamming into hers, the loud slap of his crotch against her butt signalling the finish line had been reached. He squeezed her breasts as he came, scissoring her nipples with his fingers, and pulling her toward him. She let go of the bed rail and fell back into him, letting him wrap his arms around her, before they both slumped back onto the bed.

Caleb awoke an hour later, realising he was late for work, but not particularly bothered about it. He was in too much of a good mood, and wasn't going to let work spoil things. He'd been right, sex in the morning really did set you up nicely for the day ahead. He took a shower. Got dressed, and sat on the side of the bed. He checked Jessica. She was half asleep. He kissed her on the cheek. "Got to go, Jess."

"Okay," she murmured. "Call me later."

"No problem," he said, and left the house.

Jessica got out of bed at ten, showered and had breakfast. She drove into town to do some shopping, and stopped off for a cup of coffee and a read of the newspaper. She felt so relaxed this morning that she'd clean forgotten about returning to Szabo's house to finish the job. And she was in two minds as to whether to do it at all. Now that Caleb was in her life, she was wondering if she shouldn't just forget about it completely. It had been fun whilst it lasted. Maybe it was time to let it go. But, on the other hand, the charities she had been giving the money to could always use more. And she rather liked her self image as a latter day Robin Hood.

She'd decide later. Today she would rest. She picked up the paper and took a cursory glance at the first few pages. Page five had an article on the Economic Forum, and Szabo's face was smiling out at her in a half page photo. She read it quickly, taking in the details about the new takeover battle he'd just won. Rationalisation. Efficiency savings. Greater staff productivity. All the usual buzzwords and phrases were there. Weasel words designed to hide the fact that he'd be taking over a perfectly good and profitable business, sacking half the workforce, and breaking up the company for this own profit. This guy really was pure scum.

She felt herself getting angry again, and any doubts she'd had about leaving Szabo alone disappeared. She'd remove what she could from his Lodge, and, at least, score some sort of symbolic victory over this reptile.

She gathered her things and went home. She had planning to do.

Chapter 6

Thursday arrived. Jessica ran to pick up the phone in the lounge. "Hello."

"Hi. It's me."

"Hi. Where are you?"

"In the middle of town. It's crazy down here."

"President's visit?"

'Yeah. The Secret Service have got just about every road blocked off. And he hasn't even arrived yet."

"What time's he due?"

"Late morning."

"Guess you're gonna be busy all day, then?"

"Be lucky if I get off duty by midnight. Why? You missing me?"

"Of course. I was kind of hoping for a repeat of Tuesday."

"Me too, Honey," said Caleb. "Tomorrow night. I promise."

"I guess I can wait, then"

"I hope you can. What are you going to get up to tonight?"

"What do you mean?" said Jessica.

"Nothing. Just wondering, that's all."

"I'll probably watch a movie. Since I'm all by myself, here."

"Reminds me, remember to turn the burglar alarm on, and lock all the doors and windows."

"You thinking about the thief."

"Uh-huh."

"I'll be okay."

"I know you will honey. But better to be safe than sorry."

"What if he does come?"

"Give me a call."

"You going to be able to respond?"

"Might be a bit slower than normal, with all the road blocks. But I'll make it somehow."

"Good to know."

"Okay," said Caleb. "I'll give you a call later. Check you're okay."

"Looking forward to it. You going to get intimate on the phone with me?"

"I doubt it. I figure the Secret Service will be monitoring every phone call in town today."

"Jeez. I guess you're right. I hadn't thought about that," said Jessica. "I'll speak to you later, then. Bye."

"Uh-huh," said Caleb.

Jessica put the phone down and thought about the call. She was looking forward to seeing Caleb for sure. But she was also digesting the information he'd given her. It would be a perfect night for breaking into Szabo's lodge. The presidential visit to the Economic Forum was an ideal diversion, and the Sheriff's Department were going to have more than enough to do without responding to anything else. Jessica finally made up her mind that she would do it tonight, and that it would be the last time. She didn't want to get Caleb into any trouble.

She prepared her gear for the evening and took a hot bath to relax and steady herself. The few hours before the break-in were always the most nerve wracking. Once she was on her way, the adrenaline would kick in, and she'd feel good.

She dried herself, and got dressed in her black outfit again. She left the house and made her way towards her target.

Once over the wall, she laughed to herself when she saw the same window open again. Didn't he ever close it? She used the same footholds as last time, and was on the balcony within seconds.

She knew for sure that Szabo was out, as he was delivering his speech, and she walked nimbly down the stairs to the study. She opened the top desk drawer and took out the bunch of keys that she'd seen last time. Just about to head for the door section of bookcase, she noticed a watch on the desktop. She examined it. German. Very, very expensive. Probably buy a small house with it. She put it in her backpack. That would help the charities meet their fundraising targets this month. She wondered what else he had in the strong room, if he left stuff like that hanging around on his desktop.

The bookcase door opened easily, and her torch illuminated the way to the strongroom. Once downstairs, she turned on the light and took a closer look at the electronic combination lock. It wasn't even activated. She tried the door. The handle turned, but it didn't open. She worked her way through the keys one by one until she came to one which looked about the right size for the lock. She put it in and turned it. She heard the barrels rotate and slide in place. It was open. She re-tried the handle, and this time it opened. This was so easy. Szabo was either so arrogant he didn't think that anyone would break into his house, or he just didn't care. He had so much money, if he lost a few things, it didn't matter.

The door opened outwards, and Jessica pulled it towards her. She slipped into the room beyond and closed it behind her, leaving it only slightly ajar. The room was dark, and she fumbled on the wall for a light switch, which she soon found. She flicked the switch, and there was a buzzing sound as the fluorescent tubes flickered into life. Her eyes darted around the room, taking in the scene in front of her. She was dumbstruck. There were two naked men tied to different pieces of apparatus. They both looked in pretty bad shape. It was Szabo's own little S&M torture chamber.

"What the fuck…" said Jessica to herself. Her breathing suddenly becoming rapid, and her heart feeling like it was going to race out of her chest. She hadn't expected this. What was she going to do?

She edged nearer to the first piece of kit. Almost a sort of medieval rack type thing. She peered at the man bound to it. Shit. Was he dead? She hoped not. She saw some of the weals and wounds on his skin, and noticed the leather whip hanging up nearby.

A sudden anger rose up inside of her. What kind of monster was Szabo? She knew he was a slimeball and a thoroughly nasty piece of work, but she hadn't imagined that he was as bad as this.

She bent closer to the man's face to check for breathing, and she reeled back in shock as he opened his mouth. He was trying to say something.

She felt really scared and creeped out by this room and the thought of what had gone on in it. She looked at the man again.

The man strained to open his eyes, and looked at her. "He…help…me."

Jessica rolled up her ski mask, suddenly realising that a person in a ski-mask was the last thing this poor guy would want to see. She looked him in the eye and nodded. "Don't worry. I'll get you out of here."

She turned her attention to the other man, who was shackled to an iron frame. He was in just as bad a state, but was also alive.

Jessica's mind grasped for answers. What should she do?

She rushed back upstairs and brought down some water from the kitchen. She gave some to the men, and decided on her next move.

"Don't worry, guys. I'm going to get help."

She grabbed her backpack and returned to Szabo's study. She picked up the phone and made an emergency call to the Sheriff's office. She rolled her ski-mask back down, so her voice would be muffled, and she told the operator that there was an incident in the cellar at Szabo's house, and an immediate police and ambulance response was needed.

She opened the front door, ran for the wall, and was over it in almost a single leap. She ran across the hillside, keeping out of sight behind trees and bushes. She reached the safety of home, her heart racing and feeling as if she would cough it up into her mouth at any moment. She closed the door behind her and dashed to the lounge. She closed the curtains, and took off her backpack and clothes and put them on the wooden floor. She removed Szabo's watch from the backpack pocket and put it to one side. She scooped up the pack, catsuit, mask, gloves and shoes, and threw them into the fireplace. She rolled up an old newspaper, fetched a lighter from the kitchen, and set light to it. The flames slowly started to grow taller and the blaze burned brighter as everything caught fire. She threw another few small log on top and put the fire guard back.

She took the watch upstairs and hid it in her own safe in her bedroom, before heading to the bathroom, turning on the shower and letting the hot water cascade all over her. She'd wash away all traces of the disgusting, filthy Szabo.

She got out of the shower, put on a bathrobe and went back downstairs. She checked the fire, poking it a little to let the air fuel the flames. Her equipment was now mostly ashes, with just the electronic safe-cracking device barely recognisable. Another thirty minutes and it would be a molten mess.

She turned on the TV, more for comfort, that anything else. She couldn't concentrate on watching any show tonight. As the TV blinked itself on, she heard some sirens in the distance. They must be headed for Szabo's. She sat, thinking, wondering what to do with the watch. She had to get rid of it as soon as possible. The usual guy she had been using to dispose of the stolen goods was in Los Angeles, and it might look suspicious if she left town suddenly. Especially after the two men in the cellar had seen her face. If they gave a description, it might lead the police to her. She had no idea what to do. But she wouldn't panic. She'd sit tight for the next few days, and then get on a plane to LA. Say she was going to stay with a friend.

She pulled her knees up against her chest, and snuggled into the bathrobe. Despite the fire and the warm night, she felt a chill run through her. It wasn't just the fear of getting caught, it was the shock at seeing the two men in the cellar. What a creep Szabo was. She'd vaguely known that things like that went on. The extremes of the S&M scene. She just hadn't expected she'd ever witness it. If it was spoken about at all, people would tend to joke about it. But seeing it, it was definitely no laughing matter. Szabo was a complete sicko.

She stared at the flames in the fireplace, wondering whether the police were at the house yet.

Chapter 7

The response time had been slow, as Caleb had suggested it would be. The emergency services had arrived at Szabo's house half an hour after they had received the phone call, despite the fact they were only a five minute drive away.

With all the senior men on duty for the President's visit, two rookie patrol officers attended the scene, along with some paramedics from the hospital. It was a shocking introduction to police work for the two cops, and they'd quickly radioed for backup. Another twenty minutes later, Caleb arrived.

The rookie showed him down to the dungeon in the cellar and described what she'd seen when they had first gone in. The two men were now on the floor being attended to by the paramedics.

He took a deep breath, taking in the scene in all its gory detail. Whoever did this was one sick fucker. He looked at one of the men on the blanket on the floor and winced at the sight of the whip marks all over his body. He kneeled down next to him, and looked at the paramedic. "They both gonna be OK?"

"Probably. They're half starved and badly beaten up. But they'll probably make it."

"Can they talk?"

"They really need to rest right now."

"I've only got one question."

The paramedic nodded a silent OK.

Caleb caught the man's eye. "I know you're hurting pretty bad. But just tell me, who did this to you?"

The man struggled to speak.

"Take your time. All I want is a name. Just a surname will do."

"Sza…Szabo."

Caleb nodded, rose to his feet, and walked silently back to his SUV.

Szabo was on the stage, five minutes into his speech. A light-hearted opening, a few jokes, and he had the audience in the palm of his hand already. The president, in the front row, had led the laughter and the spontaneous applause.

The press photographer's flashes had illuminated the darkened hall in response to that, all of them looking for the killer photo. A close up of Szabo for the business pages. One of the president for the front page. Szabo looked like the guy who'd won the lottery. A big shit-eating grin for the TV News crews and the live streaming over the net. He was loving every minute of it. Centre stage. Mr Big.

Caleb slipped in un-noticed at the back of the auditorium, accompanied by a Secret Service agent. They talked with another agent by the door, and the three of them made their way along the side aisle towards the stage.

"You sure about this?" the lead Agent whispered to Caleb.

"Hundred percent."

"Shit," he muttered, shaking his head. "Guess we better do it then." He nodded to the second agent, who talked into a concealed mic, alerting the other Agents as to what was about to happen.

Caleb led the way. They climbed the steps on to the stage and walked over to where Szabo was standing. Caleb removed his handcuffs from his belt and approached Szabo. Szabo was aware of somebody standing next to him and he hesitated in his speech. The audience gasped. The Secret Service led the president out of the room. The pack of photographers clicked away with their cameras, scenting blood.

Caleb spoke to Szabo, the microphone picking up his words and broadcasting them throughout the hall, and to the world. "You are under arrest. You have the right to remain silent…"

He pulled Szabo's arms behind his back, handcuffed him, and led him off the stage. This was going to be the perp walk of the century.

Chapter 8

The telephone rang. Jessica woke with a start, and a feeling of dread hit her in the stomach. It was only six in the morning. Who was calling at this time? She feared she knew. She took a deep breath and answered. "Hi."

"Jessica?"

"Yeah," she replied, rubbing the sleep from her eyes. "That you Caleb?"

"Uh-huh. Sorry for calling so early, but I need to come over. Is it okay?"

"I guess so. What is it?"

"Can't speak over the phone. I'll tell you when I get there."

"It sounds bad."

"It is. There's been some real bad shit going down. I'll be right over."

"Okay. See you soon."

Jessica got up, splashed water on her face and brushed her teeth. Sitting on the edge of the bed, she looked around, and wondered if she might be sitting in a jail cell in a few hours time. She didn't know how she was going to get out of this one.

The main gate intercom sounded, and she let Caleb through. She opened the front door and he entered silently. He looked tired.

"What is it?" asked Jessica. "What's going on?"

"You seen the news today?"

"I've only just woken up."

"We made an arrest last night?"

"The burglar?"

"No."

"Who?"

"Charles Szabo."

"Charles Szabo. The financier?"

"Uh-huh."

"What for?"

"We got him on a number of charges," said Caleb, "Let's just say the guy had his own private torture chamber at his lodge."

"What?"

"Turns out he's some kind of psycho sexual pervert. Whipped the shit out of a couple of guys he met in a bar."

"You serious?"

"Absolutely."

"Well. How did he get caught?"

"Someone discovered the room, and the two victims, in the cellar, and made an anonymous call to the Sheriff's office."

"That was lucky for them. They going to be okay?"

"They'll recover."

"You taken a statement from them yet?"

"They're in hospital, but I had a brief talk with one of them."

"What did he say?"

"Didn't make much sense. He wasn't exactly lucid. Said an angel came to his rescue. An angel in black."

"Huh?"

"Yeah. I don't know what he was going on about either. The doctor said he'd probably been hallucinating."

"An angel in black? Sounds kinda weird."

"Yeah. It's been a strange night," said Caleb. "Any chance we can continue where we left off a couple of nights ago?"

"Need to relax do you?"

"Big time."

"Want this angel to stroke you to sleep?"

"I like the sound of that."

"Being stroked?"

"Makes me think of cats. Pussies."

"Pussy, huh."

"Uh-huh. You gonna wear that catsuit for me."

"Nah. Threw it away. You were right, it was a bit tight for working out."

"You thrown it away for good?"

"Yeah. It's already gone.""

"For the best, I guess."

"Why's that?" asked Jessica, not sure what Caleb was getting at.

"I prefer you without it."

"Naked, you mean?"

"Exactly."

"We better head up to bed then."

"I guess we better had," said Caleb, taking hold of Jessica's hand and leading her up the stairs.

Fertility Rites

Chapter 1

Life wasn't too bad. I was standing in the wood panelled library of a grand Victorian lodge, warming my hands by the flames licking up from the logs I'd thrown into the huge stone fireplace a few minutes before. If this was work, I could live with it.

It was two months since I'd started here, and it was certainly a change from my old life in the city. I gazed out of the window at the green fields, a stone's throw from the house. It was a quiet morning, and I'd finished the few light work duties I had for the day.

I pulled back one of the panels on the wall to reveal a shiny new wide screen TV, and jabbed the remote control nonchalantly towards it. The news was on, and with another flick of the wrist, I zapped to an obscure cable channel, just in time to catch the beginning of a badly dubbed Hungarian soap opera I'd become addicted to. It was about a landed family who'd lost their estates during the communist era, and having now regained them, were busy recreating their former aristocratic existence, complete with butlers and retainers, gamekeepers and gardeners. The *golden* son, who'd recaptured the family's former glory, had escaped Hungary during the revolution, fled to New York, married well to a supermarket heiress who was looking for a titled husband, and after she'd died in a mysterious speed boat accident on Martha's Vineyard, he had returned to the land of his birth with eight hundred million dollars in his back pocket, and a newly rekindled interest in the boar hunting and peasant whipping of his youth. Its title in English was *The Return of the Count*.

To be honest, the show was pure, Grade-A bullshit, but I kind of liked it because it reminded me a bit of my current existence, looking after this big old house and estate.

Just as the show ended, the front gate video phone buzzed and I checked the screen. A blue Toyota with the driver leaning out of the window, a baseball cap obscuring some of her face.

"Miss Morales?" I asked

"Yes," she said "Are you Dominic Cabrini?"

"That's me," I replied, "I'll open the gates. Come on in."

She nodded and drove the car slowly through the gateway as the large metal gates swung slowly inwards.

I opened the front door and waited for her to park. She got out of the car and walked towards the front steps, removing her baseball cap as she did so. Her long dark brown hair fell down over her shoulders, and she looked at me with a large open smile on her face. Jeez, she almost knocked me backwards. She was absolutely beautiful. Olive skin, large brown eyes. A gorgeous Latina.

I put out my hand to meet hers and she took it gently and gracefully. Her skin was soft and her hand delicate. We shook hands, and I think I probably held on a little too long, but I didn't want to let go.

"It's nice to meet you," she said, in no rush to break our handshake either. "You can call me Elsa."

"Elsa. Good," I said. "Most of my friends call me Nic."

"Nic. Not Dom?"

"I've been called Dom a few times, but mostly it's Nic. Although professionally, It's Dominic."

"You're an artist, aren't you?"

"Sculptor. Clay and bronze."

"The College told me a bit about you."

"All good, I hope?"

"Of course. I saw some of your work," she said. "It was great."

"In the gallery in Steamy Springs?"

"No. Online. But I'll probably have a look when I'm in town next."

"I'd be happy to show you around."

"Sounds good."

We finally unlocked hands, and I gestured for her to come in. She removed her down jacket and I hung it up for her. She was wearing close fitting jeans and a cardigan, and I couldn't help but check out her figure. Slim yet curvy. Long legs. Great butt. I wanted to take her immediately, right there on the *Welcome* mat.

I showed her through to the Library and made us both a cup of coffee. This wasn't exactly an interview, and she'd already been assigned the job of Housekeeper by the college, but in theory, as the acting majordomo of Eagle

Creek, I was meant to be her boss.

We sat down opposite each other on the large leather armchairs that were parked either side of the fire.

"The college told you a little bit about me. So, I'll fill in the rest, very briefly."

She nodded and took a sip from her cup, her full lips leaving a slight trace of gloss around the rim.

"I'm an artist. Been a professional sculptor now for about nine years, ever since I left Art School. I'm doing okay. Not in the big league. But I'm making some good sales. Getting some commissions. And I do a bit of teaching now and again."

"Did you teach at Marlow College?"

"Yeah. I wasn't on the faculty. But I gave the occasional sculpture class to the art students. A kind of guest lecturer."

"How come you ended up here in Colorado?"

"It came out of the blue, really. I was based in New York, and was travelling up to the College in Vermont about four or five times a year. I got to know a few people there, and one day they offered me this."

"What's the deal?"

"This Lodge is owned by the College. They were left it by somebody in a legacy. Years ago. One of the alumni. They use it for a few weeks a year. For academic conferences, that type of thing. The rest of the time it's mostly empty. So they need someone to look after it. Sometimes, it's someone like me. An artist, a writer, an academic. Someone like that…"

"…who could use the free board and lodgings. And plenty of time and space to be creative?"

"Exactly. In return for a few light duties, looking after the place - no more than an hour or two a day - I get to live for free in a fantastic Rocky Mountain lodge, and can spend the rest of my day working on my sculptures."

"Sounds great."

"It is. The rent on studio space in New York was really killing me. So, it's been a real Godsend to come out here."

"Don't miss the city?"

"A little. But not as much as I thought I would."

"You a native New Yorker?"

"Yeah. Italian American. New York born and bred," I replied. "You?"

"Born in LA. Spent most of my life in Colorado. A bit of a mix of Mexican and German ancestry."

I nodded, taking in everything she was telling me, determined to know this girl in every way I could. "So what made you apply for the job?"

"Same as you. I didn't really apply. I was working as a real estate agent in town. There wasn't a lot going on in the market."

"Recession?"

"Yeah. Even Steamy Springs has been affected."

"You mean ten million dollar ski lodges are now nine million dollars?"

She laughed. "You're right. It sounds crazy, but that's about the sum of it. Even the rich are keeping a tight hold of the purse strings."

"So you got laid off?"

"Not really," she said, pushing her hair behind her ear with one hand. "My boss has some kind of connection with Marlow College, and I think they asked him to find someone to do a housekeeping job. The money was good, and it sounded like it might be interesting, and so here I am."

"Great. Well, welcome. And don't think of me as a boss. I'll be in my studio most of the day. Although, this week is busy, of course."

"The conference?"

"Uh-huh. Did they tell you about it?"

"A little," she said, putting down her coffee cup and warming her hands by the fire, the days still not warm enough to do without it. "How many people?"

"There's about thirty in total. Which is near the limit, as we've got thirty two bedrooms. Not including mine. I've got a small self contained apartment at the back of the house."

And they're arriving on Friday?"

"Friday. And leaving on Wednesday," I said. "I've got the temporary staff and the caterers and cleaners booked. They'll come in as and when they're needed. They won't be living in."

"And my job is to manage them?"

"More or less. Just keep an eye on what they're doing. Make sure everything runs to schedule. Especially the big dinner they've got on Saturday night."

"Seems manageable."

"It should be. To call it a conference is a bit overblown really. It's a bunch of academics from various colleges spending a few days talking about ancient history and archaeology. Apparently it's fairly casual. Even the dinner shouldn't be too much work. It's more like a buffet. We set everything up and then leave them to it," I said. "But, remember, this is my first time as well. I've had the house to myself up until now. So we're both new to this."

"We'll make a good team."

"I think so too," I said, and felt myself becoming more and more attracted to this girl with every passing second. "Let me show you your room. I's like a luxury hotel suite. You'll love it. And then I'll give you the guided tour of the rest of the house."

Eagle Creek was a grand lodge on the valley floor about ten minutes drive out of Steamy Springs. It had been built by the cattle baron and meat canning magnate, Jeremiah Hollister, who'd made his fortune exporting corned beef all over the world Hollister had died without an heir, and in an act of great Victorian philanthropy, he'd left the Lodge and several thousand acres to the Marlow College endowment, specifying that it be used "*…by great thinkers, who might find its calm atmosphere conducive to furthering their quest for knowledge.*"

In the weeks before I'd travelled out to Colorado, I'd begun to think that this was all some weird joke being played by Marlow, and that it all seemed to good to be true. But that feeling evaporated like water on a hot skillet the moment I set eyes on Eagle Creek. It was like something from one of the paintings I'd laboriously had to copy over and over in drawing lessons. An arcadia set amongst the green foothills surrounding Steamy Springs. Its facades, in the Scottish Baronial style, with turreted towers and grand oak doorways seemed to sleep peacefully within the landscaped gardens, under a large Colorado sky.

The inside was just as spectacular. Hollister, a keen traveller, had decorated it in a myriad of styles, from Georgian aristo-castle to High Victorian Gothic, via all sorts of imported ideas from every corner of the globe. The main downstairs rooms seemed to have separate themes, each corresponding to a different part of the world where Hollister's Corned Beef had been sold. The Grand Ballroom was modelled on the one at the Maharaja of Jaipur's palace; the West Room was all Afghan rugs, floor cushions, and in the centre, a circular iron fireplace from the Nawab of Kandahar's mountain fortress; the orangery had something of the air of Singapore's Raffles Hotel; and the sweltering humidity of the permanently heated spa rooms were crystal caves of Rocky Mountain marble, steam filled through Rhodesian copper pipes. All in all, a stunning house. And all I had to do was keep it going.

My only duties were making sure the bills were paid; drawing up a schedule of maintenance for the next five years; keeping an eye on local contractors and cleaners who came in weekly to do repairs and tidy up; and managing a contract the estate had with a local rancher who rented most of the fields, and who had some sort of deal that allowed him to do logging in the forested part of the estate. The work could be wrapped up in about two hours a day, sometimes less, except for the twice yearly occasions when the lodge was used for conferences.

Rather mysteriously, a few weeks after arriving, I'd discovered, glued to the underside of one of my desk drawers, an envelope containing a few notes made by the last Lodge Manager, a retired US Army Corps of Engineers Colonel called John Decker, who'd been living here with his wife whilst he worked on a book. He had resigned unexpectedly, and now seemed to have completely disappeared. I'd wanted to ask him about various things, and had tried to contact him on the phone number given to me by Marlow College HR Department, but there was never any answer, and the email I'd sent had, so far, not received a reply. Decker's notes read like the ramblings of a paranoid personality. They were addressed to "The Next Lodge and Estate Manger of Eagle Creek" and were basically a warning that no-one could be trusted, and that there were "…weird things happening" at Eagle Creek. I didn't know what to make of it, but was inclined to ignore it, especially as Marlow College had somewhat cryptically suggested that Colonel Decker had suffered from a nervous breakdown. They'd mentioned the "…isolation of life at Eagle Creek" and "The trauma he'd suffered in Iraq."

Negotiating with the caterers had also been a pain in the butt, as the ones who had done the job in the past seemed to have gone out of business, and I was reduced to scouring the Yellow Pages to find someone else. They were local, but whether they were any good was one of my known unknowns. And with the big dinner on Saturday, I was getting kind of nervous about it.

After showing Elsa around and filling her in on the Lodge's history and briefly mentioning Colonel Decker, she wanted to see my studio and was interested in what I was working on. She had a keen interest in art, and I was rapidly starting to lose my heart to Miss Morales. I couldn't help it. Italian Americans are an emotional breed. Artists, even more so.

She followed me into the studio and immediately went over to the far end of the room to take a closer look at my latest work. She couldn't really miss it.

"It's big," she said.

"Twelve foot tall."

"What is it?"

"It's a piece I did for the college."

"It's in lieu of rent, huh?"

"Something like that. I figured I owed them something, for letting me stay here. Besides, it was great fun working on it. I've never really attempted anything so big before."

"Who's it meant to be?"

"It's a representation of the ancient Canaanite fertility goddess, Astarte."

"Fertility goddess?"

"Fertility goddess," I repeated, shrugging my shoulders. "It's a bit different from my usual stuff, but I've always been influenced by the art of the ancient world."

"The College wanted you to do this?"

"They said they wanted a statue of Astarte. But they left me to interpret it how I wanted."

"Why do they want a statue of an ancient goddess?"

"History, archaeology, classics. Those are their big subjects. What they're renowned for. They've got a whole load of art and antiquities in the college library and museum. And this place is full of the stuff."

"Hmm. Are you into this type of thing?"

"What? Fertility goddesses?"

"Yeah?"

"I didn't know anything much about it until I started on this. But it's been interesting doing the research."

"So what's she meant to do? Ensure the success of the harvest?"

"That type of thing," I said, starting to feel a little foolish and wondering whether Elsa thought I was a weirdo. "The ancients prayed to her for the fertility of the land, and for themselves."

"Themselves?"

"Yeah. I don't know exactly. But she's one of these all encompassing mother goddesses. Goddess of fertility, love, sex, procreation. You name it."

"Does it work?"

"What?"

"Are her powers for real?"

"Who the hell knows. Some people believe it, I guess."

Elsa nodded as if deep in thought. "No harm in trying I suppose." She kneeled down in front of the statue, clasped her hands together, and seemed to mutter something.

"What did you pray for?"

"That would be telling."

"Fair enough. Let me know if it comes true, though."

"Why? You going to try it yourself?"

"No. I'll start admitting the public. Hundred bucks a prayer. I'll clean up."

"You should have become a salesman instead of an artist."

"Unfortunately, you've got to be both to make it in the art world these days. In fact, you need ninety percent selling skills, ten percent art skills."

"After seeing some of the stuff that sells for a million dollars, you're probably right."

"I think so," I said. "You want to have a go?"

"At what?"

"Art. A bit of clay sculpture."

"I'd love to. What do I do?"

"Come over here," I said, and I led her to the work table.

She removed her cardigan and placed it on a chair. She was wearing a close fitting shirt, and she rolled up the sleeves. I noticed the shape of her breasts against the cotton, and I felt my cock stirring to life. She looked so damn cute. All dark tumbling hair and olive skin. Rounded curves and lithe limbs. She was a goddess herself.

"How do I start?"

"Just put your hands on the piece of clay in front of you, and mould it into the shape you want to make. Don't worry too much about it at the moment. Just get a feel for the clay. See what you can do with it."

She flexed her fingers and started to work the clay. Squeezing and pinching, and smoothing it with her palms. Playing with it. Exploring its possibilities. "Feels good."

"Does, doesn't it." I said. "It's therapeutic. Good stress-buster."

"I bet."

"What are you going to make?"

"No idea. I'll just see what emerges," she said, and began to shape the clay into a kind of tower, running her palms along the length of it, slowly making it bigger and bigger.

Watching her work the clay was killing me. My erection was just about bursting out of my pants and I was wishing it was her hands running along the shaft of my cock, instead of the sculpture.

"I think it's going to collapse any second," she said. "Help."

Fuck me, I thought, *it's the opposite of my tower, then.* I moved behind her, took hold of her hands and helped her stabilise the clay. We stood back and looked at her work of art, my hands still on hers, our clay covered fingers now interlaced.

"What do you think?" she asked me.

"It's good. For a five minute first effort, it's not too bad at all."

"Thank you," she said. "You know this is the second time since we met an hour ago that you've held my hand."

"I know. I'm kind of tactile, I guess. I am a sculptor."

"You're good with your hands then?"

"Years of practice."

"Want to show me," she said, removing her hands from mine, placing them either side of my face and drawing my mouth towards hers.

Jeez, she doesn't waste much time. "My pleasure," I managed to mutter before our lips met. The feel and taste of her instantly shot me full of adrenalin and I encircled her waist and held her next to me. My cock pressed against the front of her jeans. Only denim between us. I moved my hand on to her butt, and took in its full, perfect roundness. Neither too soft nor too hard. Just right. Shapely and sexy and utterly wonderful.

We parted briefly, so I could remove her shirt. I threw it to one side, and unhooked her bra. She responded by tugging my T-shirt off me, and I pulled us firmly back together, where our naked flesh met, the warmth and softness of her breasts against my chest. I cupped her tits in my hands and played with her nipples, leaving traces of clay across her skin. "I want to cover your naked body with this stuff from head to toe."

"Is that the kind of kinky stuff sculptors get up to?"

"You better believe it."

"Go ahead," she said. "As long as I get to do the same to you."

I grunted a reply as I lifted her on to the bench and removed her jeans and panties, and somehow managed to kick off my sneakers and shimmy out of my own jeans.

Elsa grabbed my erection with one hand, took a lump of clay with the other and began to smear it all over my cock.

I followed her lead, and began to rub the warm, wet clay on her breasts and down onto her tummy, the both of us laughing as we massaged it into each other.

I looked into her eyes, and kissed her. "The moment you stepped up to the front door, I wanted you."

"I know. I felt the same about you."

"Love at first sight, huh?"

"Could be. Or maybe it's the work of your goddess there."

"The goddess of love brought us together. Maybe this stuff is true after all," I said. "Is that what you prayed for?"

"If I tell you it might break the spell."

"Wouldn't want to do that," I said, as my lips began their descent down her body, brushing lightly against her hip bone before curving inwards until I reached the sweet smelling and welcoming land between her legs. I looked at her beautiful mound of Venus and glanced quickly at the statue of Astarte smiling down benignly on us, some part of my mind aware of the goddess connection. I couldn't stand the wait any longer and I buried my face in her vulva, its slick folds yielding to my tongue and giving up its precious nectar. The drink of the gods. And the goddesses.

Chapter 2

After me and Elsa had made out in the studio, including making good on my promise to cover her all over in clay, we went to the spa rooms to clean up. We took a shower together and washed the clay from each other's bodies. I lathered up some gel between my hands and ran my palms over her, along the gentle slope of her shoulders, down the graceful arch of her back, and out over her hips and butt. As her clean, golden flesh was, revealed from beneath the earth-brown clay, I kissed her gently, wrapped my arms around her, and stroked and teased her neat little triangle of hair, my fingers gently prising apart her thighs. She shuddered slightly as my fingertips fleetingly stroked her swollen clit, her muscles tensing and then relaxing again as I moved them onwards and along the opening of her pussy. I curled my fingers upwards and pushed into her, entering her smoothly. She sighed contentedly as I stroked the inside of her vagina, several fingers now within, and giving her a satisfying feeling of fullness.

She placed both her palms against the shower wall to steady herself and began to move her hips rhythmically,   enabling my fingers to move in and out of her with ease. I kneeled down behind her and she rode my fingers for a while, my other hand caressing her thigh, and my lips now kissing her butt. She began to move faster, wanting to be penetrated deeper and harder, but frustrated that my fingers couldn't quite satisfy her enough. I rose to my feet, opened her legs a little wider, and glided my cock into her. It met no resistance, and I filled her completely, her honey-juiced pussy sliding freely along the length of my cock, yet gripping me tightly, like two precision made machine parts that were a perfect fit for each other.

I held on to her hips and began to pump in and out rapidly, burying my cock fully inside her. I moved my hands upwards, fondling her breasts and tweaking her nipples. I kissed her shoulders and the back of her neck as I pulled her on to me again and again.

Her moans of pleasure became louder as we hurried towards climax, both needing the sweet release of orgasm. I thrust into her again. Almost there. She moved her hands behind her and grasped for my butt, trying to pull me further in, wanting every inch. Our minds now frenzied, our breathing rapid, we finally came, her with a shriek, and me with a low satisfied groan as my juice flowed into her, like an accelerant igniting a fire inside, that spread throughout her entire body, engulfing her in pleasure.

We slumped onto the cubicle floor and held each other for a while, letting ourselves relax in the warm steam filled shower, enjoying the feel of each other's wet body against our own.

I got up first and led Elsa to the large sunken bath that sat in the middle of the grand spa room. The walls were tiled with mosaics depicting classical scenes from an orgy, highly sexual images of men and women frolicking and fucking at the Roman baths. Their faces happily innocent and free of any shame or guilt. Enjoying the pleasures of the flesh, naturally and instinctively.

We sat contentedly next to each other, immersed up to our chests in the hot waters, marvelling at the decoration, and making small talk.

"Who designed the mosaics?" she said.

"The guy who built the place. Hollister. Apparently he'd studied Ancient History at Marlow."

"Did he get up to any of this stuff, or is it purely a work of the imagination?"

"By all accounts, he was a bit of a sexual athlete. I think if these walls could speak, they'd have a few stories to tell about the parties Hollister used to hold here."

"What sort of thing?"

"I don't know that much, but from what I was told by one of the Professor's at Marlow, the guy had more than his fair share of women."

"Wasn't he married?"

"He was. And openly he lived a respectable everyday life. Rich businessman. Pillar of the community."

"His wife didn't mind?"

"I don't know if she knew. She never lived here. She stayed back East. One of the Carolinas, where they had another estate. She couldn't stand the cold and the isolation here. It was just him who used to come for months at a time."

"She thought he was managing his businesses?"

"I guess that's right. And he was. But he was obviously getting up to all sorts of other stuff as well."

"Didn't they have any children?"

"No. That was the thing, you see. He couldn't have any kids. He was infertile. He thought it was his wife at first, and that's why he started sleeping with other women. He was desperate for an heir to inherit the family fortune."

"But still no kid, even with the mistresses?"

"Right. So that's when he started getting into this ancient fertility rites business. Gods, goddesses, you name it. There's pagan symbolism all over the Lodge. Carvings, paintings. If you look at the mosaic there, you'll see Venus," I said, pointing to some figures on the wall. "And that's Ceres, an agricultural deity. And that guy over the end there. Did you spot him? Can't really miss him, can you? The guy with the huge boner. That's Priapus."

Elsa looked over and giggled. "He's a big boy, huh?"

"Too big by the look of him. He'd probably split you in half with that thing."

"Might be fun trying though."

"Like them big, do you?"

"Don't get insecure, Nic. You're big enough."

"Nice to hear it."

"How do I measure up to Venus?"

"You could have been the model for that mosaic."

"Flattery will probably get you everywhere. You hoping to get inside my panties again later today?"

"Absolutely."

"Honesty as well as flattery."

"They're good qualities."

"They are," she said, stroking my chest and putting her head on my shoulder. "I guess they're a few of the reasons I like you so much."

I beamed a big grin and started to slowly submerge myself in the water.

"Where you going?"

"I hear there's a beautiful underwater cave in these parts," I said , putting on my Pirates of the Caribbean accent. "With a nice shiny pearl waiting for those who venture there."

"You gonna steal the pearl?"

"I'll just play around with it for a while."

My head sank below the water line, and I headed for the treasure.

"Oh my God…" said Elsa, as I pushed between her legs. "That's good…"

Chapter 3

After we'd left the spa room, Elsa left to go back to her apartment to pick up some of her things. She was going to be living in for the duration of the conference, and was going to pack a couple of suitcases. I kissed her goodbye at the door, sad to see her leaving , even though she'd be back this evening.

"I'll miss you."

"I'll miss you too."

"Maybe, I'll cook us a nice dinner tonight."

"You like to cook?"

"Of course. I'm Italian," I said. "I'll think about what to eat and head to the store later. I'll get some wine, too."

"Sounds great," said Elsa. "What else are you doing?"

"I've got to head up to see the guy who farms some of the estate for us. Bill Brockley."

"Are you going to be a cowboy for the afternoon?"

"Nothing so enjoyable," I said. "Yesterday, a truck full of chemical fertiliser was delivered here. It was meant to be delivered to his ranch."

"You want him to come around and move it?"

"No. I didn't allow them to unload it. It's gone back to the warehouse."

"Why?"

"Well in the contract we have with him, he's meant to be farming the estate organically. So none of this chemical crap is allowed."

"So, you're going to talk to him about it?"

"Yeah. Just tell him what happened, and not to use that stuff."

"What's he like?"

"I've only met him two or three times. He seems okay , I guess."

"Well be careful. Don't get into a fight."

"Don't worry. He's not violent. Or, at least, I hope he's not."

"Okay. See you later."

"Bye," I said. We kissed again, and she left. I opened the front gates for her, and then I grabbed my coat and keys, and jumped into my SUV.

Brockley's ranch was just a ten minute drive away, and I used the time to figure out what I was going to say to him. I'd not really told the truth to Elsa.

He was a difficult character. Independent, stubborn, the last of the rugged individualists. He wasn't the sort of person who'd take kindly to me telling him how to run his ranch. Even if he was renting our land. Contract, or no contract.

I pulled up outside the main house and knocked on the front door. Brockley answered, put a coat on, and gestured for us both to take a walk.

"What can I do for you, Nic?"

"There's something I need to discuss with you."

"Go ahead."

"There was a delivery of chemical fertiliser delivered to Eagle Creek yesterday," I said, watching his face to see if it betrayed what he was thinking. "I sent it back to the warehouse."

"I wondered where that had got to," he said.

"So, you ordered it?"

"Of course I did, son."

"You know that under the terms of your contract you're not supposed to be using chemicals on our land. It's strictly organic."

"I wasn't going to use it on Eagle Creek's land. I was going to use it on my own land."

"So, it's just for your ranch, not the land you rent from us?"

"That's right," he said.

"So why was it delivered to us. The delivery note said that it was to be delivered to Eagle Creek Estate?"

"Must be a mistake. Those boys down at the agricultural suppliers know I rent land from you as well as farming my own. They've got themselves mixed up."

"Okay. I know I don't know anything about farming, but don't you use your land for the ranching? Cattle farming? And don't you use our land for growing crops?"

"That's about right," said Brockley. "What's your point, son?"

"Well, Fertiliser suggests that you're putting it on the land for crops, not on the land for cattle."

A rictus grin spread across Brockley's face. "You're right son. You don't know anything about farming. That was just a few sacks of lime. Don't go worrying yourself about it."

"So. You're not using it on our land?" I pressed him for a straight answer.

"Look son. I don't like being told how to run my farm, and if I say I'm doing things the right way, then I'm doing them the right way. I don't want my word questioned. Especially by some city boy."

"I'm not here to cause you any trouble. I'm just trying to make sure that the terms of the contract are being adhered to. You've got an amazingly good value contract. You won't find any cheaper land to rent."

"You looking to renegotiate?"

"No," I said. "I just need to check you're not doing something you shouldn't. As far as I'm aware the College have no plans to change the contract."

"There won't be any change in the contract. You can be sure of that," said Brockley.

"Why's that?"

"I get such a good deal on account of the little jobs I perform for the college from time to time."

"Like what?"

"Doesn't matter. You'll find out soon enough."

I had no idea what he was talking about, and I was getting fed up of his evasive answers and veiled threats. He was up to something, I was sure of it. I just didn't know what. "Okay, I've said my piece. As long as we're both aware of what we should and shouldn't be doing."

"I know my rights."

"Okay. And whilst I'm here, can you tell me what you're up to in the forest?"

"Cutting down a few trees."

"You're aware that ninety percent of it is for preservation?"

"I am," he said, "And, I'm only cutting down a small area every year, and then replanting."

"So, you're planting more than you're cutting down?"

"A lot more," he said, "Look son, if you've got something to say, just spit it out."

"I've got nothing to say. But I might take a walk up there later. Just see what's been going on."

"You won't find nothing. Wasting your time."

"Yeah," I said. "Look, I've got to go. I've got to prepare for the conference."

"Friday isn't it?"

"How do you know?"

"Same time every year. Start of Spring. The snow melts, the Professor's arrive. Regular as clockwork"

"But how do you know it's Friday?"

"I've got my sources," he said, tapping the side of his nose with his finger. "I know what's going on."

I mumbled a reply, too tired of our conversation to talk any longer. I nodded him farewell, walked back to the SUV, and drove back to Eagle Creek.

I stopped at the store on the way back and bought enough food and wine to keep us going for a few days. Back at the lodge I went to the kitchen, turned on the radio, got myself a beer from the cooler and started to prepare something for dinner. My talk with Brockley had left me in bad mood. He was a really difficult guy, and I hated dealing with him. I was also a bit disconcerted that he knew about the conference. Was he in touch with someone from Marlow? Was he now going to call them and complain about me? It was all a pain in the ass. Apart from him, the job was fine, but on days like this it left me feeling like not wanting to do any of my real work. I'm not the particularly sensitive type of artist. The one who can only work when inspired, or when the muse arrives. I usually just get down to it. But sparring with Brockley always seemed to drain my energy, and I never got any good work done after it. Experience told me it was best to have a nice meal, a few drinks, some good company and then a good night's sleep. And that's exactly what I had lined up for the evening. Although, hopefully, there wouldn't be too much sleeping going on in the bed tonight.

Chapter 4

I woke up next to Elsa and pulled her closer. She was already awake, and seemingly ready to take on the day's challenges. I, on the other hand, wasn't really a morning person, and I liked to lie around in bed for a while before getting up.

She ran her hand over my chest and kissed my cheek. I patted her butt and stroked along the line of her hips and onto her waist. Although I was sleepy, my cock had its own agenda, and it sprang to life, standing to attention at the feel of Elsa's warm thigh against it.

"Your little soldier ready for action again?"

"Looks like it," I said.

"Feels like it to. All pumped up and ready to go."

"He's keen."

"No point hanging around then," she said, and she took hold of my cock and squeezed it.

I lay back and let out a deep sigh of contentment. Could life be any better. Waking up next to the woman of my dreams in a beautiful lodge in the Rocky Mountains.

Elsa was obviously in no mood for messing around and she lifted herself up and straddled me. Her smooth tanned thighs gripped tightly against my hips, her perky breasts bounced around merrily in front of me, and her pussy hovered teasingly above my cock.

I gripped her butt with both hands and manoeuvred her closer. My cock brushed fleetingly across the length of her vulva, searching for the entrance, but not quite finding it.

Elsa giggled. "You want to come in?"

"Nowhere else I want to be right now."

"Can you find your way?"

"Let me have another go." I said, and I moved her onto me again. This time, I found her holy of holies.

Elsa moaned as the head of my cock wriggled it's way slowly into her. Her vaginal lips opened briefly, but for just long enough, before closing again around me, gripping me tight.

I began to lift my hips off of the bed and move them in a thrusting motion, trying to burrow deeper inside her. She was nicely wet, and my cock glided in and out of her smoothly.

Elsa moved in her own circular motion, and it took a few moments before we recognised each other's rhythm and were able to move as one.

She liked my cock to touch the front wall of her vagina, each thrust sending waves of pleasure through her. I responded by pushing harder, aiming each time for that little spot that seemed to send her crazy. Each time I hit it, I felt her tighten a little more around me, and her whole body tensed up, before once again relaxing as I withdrew.

I kept one hand on her butt cheek, and moved my other one up to her breasts, cupping one of them, feeling its weight and form, fascinated how it felt and how it moved.

Her movement never stopped, and she kept on riding the length of my cock, heading purposefully to the land of the Big O. It was close now, and like a marathon runner sighting the finish line, her body surged full of adrenalin and found the energy to sprint to the finish.

I knew where she was going, and I was heading there too. My hand returned to her butt. I needed something to grip on to. Like a plane coming in to land, the last few minutes of this ride were going to be bumpy.

We thrust against each other almost violently now, with me trying to control her movements as much as I could. I caressed the roundness of her bottom before once again gripping her hips tightly.

Her hands were on my chest, her fingers kneading my skin, looking for something to grasp, something to brace herself against, so that she might better cope with the lightning bolt that was about to strike her. We were creating so much electrical charge between us, we could have powered the town for the next half hour.

I felt myself about to come. The familiar feeling of my juice rising from my balls and beginning it's ascent up my cock. I bit my lip, trying to hold it in for a moment longer. I looked at Elsa, and she seemed to gesture silently that it would just be another few seconds, and then we could both allow ourselves to succumb to the pleasure and release of orgasm.

I held her tighter, and her movements became more erratic, her body shuddering, unable to take any more. She had to come.

I pushed inside her one last time, and I was done. I let out a deep breath as my cum flowed out into her, and I pulled her hard onto me, not wanting even a hair's breadth between or bodies.

Elsa flung back her head as she came, her muscles tautening wildly as if in spasm, before finally slumping forward and on to me. Her head nuzzled in to my neck, her silky hair splayed across my face, her arms wrapped around me.

We kissed and stroked each other and uttered loving words in each other's ear. My mind was frenzied, and yet somehow at the same time calm, and I knew for certain, as sure as I'd ever known anything in my life, that I was in love with this woman. It seemed crazy. I'd only known her a day. But I was one hundred percent, totally in love.

We kissed and cuddled some more, talked about the day ahead, and about a half hour later we got up, showered together, and dressed.

It was going to be a busy day. Tomorrow was Friday. The start of the conference, and there were a million little things to do, check and double check. I didn't know if we'd have time for sex again today, but when I looked at Elsa, shimmying herself into the cutest little pair of panties, I figured we could probably find time in our schedule. Making love with this girl was the priority. Work could always wait.

Chapter 5

I went downstairs and fixed us both some breakfast, had a quick look at the TV news, and wandered down the driveway to get the mail.

The mail box had a few junk mailshots and a solitary letter. The return address written in blue ink on the back said "Decker" and gave an address in Oregon. So, the Colonel had finally gotten around to contacting me, had he? I ran my finger along the flap and took the letter out of the envelope. I read it on the way back to the house, completely engrossed, not noticing the fine spring morning that was happening around me. The sun warmed my skin, but I felt cold all over. The contents of the letter chilled me to the bone.

I slumped onto a chair in the kitchen and took a big gulp of coffee. Elsa was nibbling on some pastries and looked over at me.

"Bad news?"

"Possibly. I don't know what to make of it," I said, massaging the back of my neck. "It's about Decker."

"The guy who ran the house before you."

"Yeah. Colonel Decker."

"He finally got in touch?"

"No," I said. "It's not from him. It's from his sister in Portland."

"His sister," said Elsa, her brain ticking over. "Oh my God. He hasn't passed away has he?"

"No. Not so far as I can tell. It's almost worse than that."

"Worse?"

"Yeah," I said, shifting uncomfortably on the wooden chair. "He's missing."

"Missing?"

"Right. She says in the letter that him and his wife haven't been seen since in months."

"Jeez. Didn't you say that he had some mental problem."

"That's what the college hinted at, yeah."

"You don't think he's done something stupid?"

"Who knows. They said he'd suffered some kind of breakdown on account of what he'd witnessed in Iraq."

"Do you think he was unstable enough to…"

"I don't know. But even if he was, I don't know whether his wife was."

"You hear of these suicide pacts."

"It's possible. But if they did something like that, where the hell are the bodies?"

Elsa nodded her head, as if mulling over everything. "When were they last seen?"

"Again, I don't know," I said. "I don't really know anything."

"Are you going to reply to his sister?"

"I guess so. But there's not much I can tell her. I'll just express my concern, and hope that they show up soon."

"How did she know to write to you?"

"She managed to access his emails somehow. Saw my email with my contact details."

"I could ask some questions, if you like?"

"To who?"

"I know a couple of guys in the Sheriff's Office in Steamy Springs. See if they know anything."

"I don't know," I said. "I'm not sure we should get involved in this."

"It'll only take an hour or so."

I thought about it for a moment. "Okay. You go into town. But make sure you're back by lunchtime at the latest. We've got a whole lot of stuff to do."

"Okay," said Elsa, a glint in her eye.

I noticed the enthusiasm with which she mentioned doing some investigation, and I wondered if she was interested in doing that type of work. She'd been a real estate agent, and in my way of thinking people who made good real estate agents would probably make a good PI. They loved snooping around other people's property. She was smart and streetwise, as well as beautiful, and I figured she'd make a sexy Private Eye. Not that I knew much about that world. I guess I was just thinking about TV shows and movies, and I had a happy little thought about her being a Charlie's Angels type character. I felt a smile creep across my face.

She looked at me curiously. "What are you grinning at?"

"Nothing," I said "Just a little fantasy playing inside my head. Maybe I'll tell you later."

"What does it involve? Me?"

"Yeah. Just you, me, and some handcuffs."

"Handcuffs. You better tell me *all* about it later."

"I promise," I said. "But right now I've got to get some work done."

"Okay. I'll be back soon," said Elsa, picking up her coat and keys. She left the kitchen, still chewing on a Danish, and muttering to herself "Handcuffs, huh?"

I spent the rest of the morning giving orders to the cleaners, maids, and porters who'd been hired to prepare the house ready for the conference. The lodge was cleaned by a gang of twelve from top to bottom, beds were made, furniture moved, food and drinks were delivered, audio-visual equipment was set up, trash was removed. Everything was done to make sure the delegates would have a comfortable and enjoyable few days. And enough provisions brought in so that the conference could take place in peace and quiet without too many interruptions.

Most of them would be here tomorrow. They were flying in to Denver from all over the country, and a few from overseas, before then being brought by airport bus to Steamy Springs. Professor Charles of Marlow College, the conference organiser, was arriving tonight. He had preparations to make.

I was planning on keeping out of the way for most of the conference. I quite liked the idea of me and Elsa hiding away together in bed for five days. Only venturing out of my apartment when my pager sounded or my cell rang. But on the other hand, I was quite curious to hear what they were discussing, and maybe listen to some of the lectures. Professor Charles had indicated that I could sit on some sessions, but others, especially the dinner on Saturday, were definitely private. I had asked him, jokingly, what the secrecy was all about, and he mentioned something about it being a bit like the Skull and Bones at Yale, and how their Society had their own "charming little customs." Just a bit of fun, he said. I don't know whether that was meant to satisfy my curiosity, but it didn't. I was even keener to know what they were getting up to. I was always amused by grown adults, usually men, joining organisations like the Freemasons, and I imagined them wearing some ridiculous regalia and reciting ancient oaths. It wasn't my scene, but there was no accounting for taste.

Elsa got back just in time for lunch, and I made us both a sandwich and got some sodas from the refrigerator. I closed the kitchen door to block the noise of the cleaners still vacuuming downstairs, and we sat opposite each other at the table. "Any luck?"

"I spoke to Caleb Blake. He's one of the Detectives at the Sheriff's Office. Nice guy."

"He know anything?"

"No. He didn't know anything about it. But he went to check with some of the other Detectives. And guess what?"

Slightly startled, I took a swig of soda to wash my sandwich down, worried that I might choke on it when I'd heard what she was going to say. "Don't tell me they've found some bodies."

"No," said Elsa, who looked like she was enjoying this. "The mystery deepens."

"What?"

"Turns out they weren't the first people to disappear in Steamy Springs."

"What? You're saying there's a serial killer on the loose?"

"Could be. But the guys at the Sheriff's Office became real cagey all of a sudden. I had to prod them for answers."

"They're keeping something quiet?"

"Apparently, there's been a random series of missing persons cases going back a few decades. Maybe five or six in total over the years. But the investigation has always come to a dead end. The Sheriff's Office don't know whether its just some weird coincidence or whether it something more."

"There's a pattern though, right? Otherwise, they wouldn't be investigating this type of thing. People go missing all the time. It's a free country, You can't keep tabs on everyone."

"Yeah. Exactly, there's a pattern," said Elsa. "The people who went missing were always couples. A man and a woman. Three cases were in the spring time. Three in the fall. When did Decker and his wife disappear?"

"Would have been around October, I think."

"When did you arrive."

"I started In January. The job had been vacant for a few months then.

Some security company from town were keeping an eye on this place."

"Didn't you mind being in this big old house by yourself."

"Yeah, I was a bit spooked when I first came. But, I soon got used to it. I quite like the peace and quiet," I said, "What are you getting at? You think Decker and his wife are buried under the floorboards?"

"Not exactly, but when you take into account Decker's notes that you found, it's kind of strange, don't you think?"

"Coincidence, maybe," I said. "None of the other disappearances had any connection to Eagle Creek did they?"

"Not directly, no. But one of the couples worked for a catering company who used to occasionally do work here."

"The catering companies in town probably do work for every lodge owner in Steamy Springs. There's plenty of rich people here who don't want to do their own cooking, especially if they've got a big party on. It's that kind of resort town."

"You're right, but there is a slight connection, isn't there?"

"Yeah. I admit there is a tiny connection, but nothing to worry about," I said. "Besides, I had some friends up from New York a few weeks ago. With their pet dog. It's a hound. If there were anything buried in the house or garden, he'd have sniffed it out."

"You're probably right," said Elsa. "It's just sort of creepy thinking that someone's disappeared from the face of the earth."

"Could be alien abduction," I said.

Elsa laughed. "How far are we from Roswell here?"

"Not far enough if they're travelling by flying saucer."

"Maybe Decker was working on top secret stuff when he was in the military."

"Yeah, he was in the Engineers. Do you think he was reverse engineering a UFO?"

"You've been watching too much daytime cable."

"Sad, but true," I said, shaking my head. "Anyway, wherever Colonel and Mrs Decker are, I hope they're okay. But, unfortunately, we've got a conference to prepare for right now."

"You're right. Let's finish as as soon as we can and then watch some of those trashy shows on TV, with a bottle of wine, in front of the fire.

"Sounds good," I said. "You make sure the cleaners have done a good job, and I'll check on the guy rigging up the audio-visual. Meet back here to go over the schedule in an hour."

"Aye, aye Captain," said Elsa, saluting me.

I groaned. "If I carry on giving orders, you have permission to shoot me."

"Noted," she said, and headed out of the kitchen.

I went to the grand ballroom, which now had a large rectangular conference table in the middle of it. Enough to seat thirty easily. The blackout curtains on the windows had been drawn, so the technician could test the screen and make sure it could be comfortably seen by everyone, and there was no glare from the lights, or daylight creeping in from outside. I stood in the doorway watching him.

"Can you flick the light switch?" he asked me.

I turned off the lights and the room was in darkness apart from the glow from the large screen, currently showing a demo video. I marvelled at how effective the blackout curtains were, and wondered whether I should get some for my bedroom, especially with summer coming up. I hated being woken at dawn by the rising sun.

"How does it look to you?"

"Looks good," I said. "Like being at the movie theatre."

"Yeah. I think it's okay too," he said. "Finally. It took a long time to set up."

"You finished now?"

"Just got the Broadband connection to do."

"You using wireless?"

"I tried it. The walls in this goddamn house are so thick, the reception is really bad. I'm going to have to run a cable in from somewhere. They don't build 'em like this any more."

"They don't," I agreed. "I don't know what they've done in previous years. Maybe they didn't bother with the internet."

"It was the same last year. I thought they might have had things sorted out by now."

"You were here last year?"

"Yeah. I've been doing these conferences here for the last three years."

"You must have known Colonel Decker, then."

"I knew Decker. Great guy. Lovely wife, as well."

"Really. I heard he was a little bit...uptight," I said, grasping for a word that wouldn't convey too much.

"Decker. No. Well not at first, anyway," said the technician. "He started getting a bit agitated around the time of the last conference. I think it was quite stressful. He was working on his book at the same time."

"I heard he was writing. Any idea what he was working on?"

"Something to do with Iraq. That's why he got a bit emotional. I think it brought up a lot of bad memories."

"I can imagine," I said. "What happened to him? Why did he leave?"

"I heard that he finished the book, and him and his wife went to Hawaii. They got fed up of the cold here."

"Who told you that?"

"Bill Brockley."

"Brockley. You know him?"

"Yeah. I see him around from time to time. He's a regular at a couple of the bars that I drink at."

"Why was he talking about Decker?"

"Just chatting, you know," said the technician. "Brockley's always real interested in what's going on here at the lodge."

"Is he?"

"Yeah. Because of him renting the land, I guess. Maybe he's thinking of making an offer for the place. The College use it so rarely. Just a few times a year. I think old Bill wouldn't mind buying the place for himself. Expand his empire."

"I can't see the college selling it," I said. "Besides, I think there's some sort of clause in Hollister's will that means that the College aren't able to sell it."

"He was a strange one, huh?" said the technician. "Jeremiah Hollister?"

"You seen all the mosaics and paintings around the house?"

"I sure have. Makes you wonder what he was getting up to all those years ago," he said "But I was thinking more of the vault under the house."

"Vault?" I said. "What vault?"

The technician smiled. He was pleased that he'd been able to surprise me. "Yeah. I didn't know anything about it either, until last year, when I tried running a cable in here. I ended up following a whole load of other cables into the basement. I couldn't figure where they were going. Eventually, me and Decker found our way down to another level below the basement."

"Another level underground?"

"Yeah. Real spooky it was. Like a crypt in some horror movie."

"Was there anything in there?"

"Lots of strange shit. Statues, mosaics on the walls. You wouldn't believe it."

"What happened?"

""We got out pretty quick. Decker told me not to say anything. Said something about it confirming his suspicions."

"What did he mean?"

"Don't know. But I guess he was thinking that Hollister had been a strange guy."

"Have you been back down there?"

"No way. I keep my nose out of these things. This is a pretty good contract I've got here. Only a few days work a year and they pay me a shit load of money for it. They don't want me to go down there. I won't. They want me to keep my mouth shut. I will."

"You told me, though."

"I figured you're one of them, aren't you. Like Decker."

"How do you mean?"

"You've been hired by Marlow to run this place. I just figured they must consider you trustworthy."

I nodded. I guessed everyone in town did see me as a 'Marlow man'. Why would they think I was anything different? "I work for them. But I'm not really one of them," I said, keen to distance myself for some reason, but not entirely sure why I said it. "And I didn't know about the vault. I thought I'd seen everything in this house. Can you show me?"

"I don't know. I don't want to get into trouble," he said, suddenly unsure of himself.

"Well, I am the Manager of this place," I said.

He thought for a moment, "Okay then. Don't suppose it will do any harm. Since it's you asking."

I followed him out of the door, and we bumped into Elsa in the hallway.

"Where are you two going?"

I beckoned with my finger for her to join us. "Follow me."

She looked intrigued, and the three of us headed towards the basement.

Chapter 6

Once down in the basement, the technician rolled back the linoleum floor covering in one corner, revealing the stone tiling. One section of the tiles was loose, and he was able to pull it upwards. It was a trapdoor.

I grabbed a flashlight from a shelf and shone it downwards. There was a stone stairway. I went down first, followed by Elsa, and finally the technician.

I realised that we were in some sort of ante-chamber, and straight in front of us was a double-width doorway with a heavy black curtain drawn across it. I looked at Elsa, "This is some spooky shit."

"I know. I'm kind of scared about what we're going to find in there."

"Only one way to find out, I guess."

"After you," said Elsa.

"Thanks. Shouldn't it be ladies first?"

"Normally. But not in this case," she replied.

I took a deep breath, pulled back the curtain and went through the doorway. I felt like Howard Carter peering into Tutenkhamen's tomb for the first time. I just hoped there was no curse.

The beam from the flashlight illuminated different sections of the vault as I moved it along the walls. I jumped slightly as faces on the walls seemed to stare back at me. "Jeez," I said. "What the hell is this place?"

Elsa was virtually speechless. "It's creepy. I don't like it."

"I told you it was weird down here," said the technician.

"Is there any electric light?" I asked

"I think there was a small light somewhere, but it wasn't working the last time I was here. I think it must have been lit by candles in the past."

We explored some more, looking at the various pictures on the walls and the large statues glaring down at us. I had no idea what most of this shit was, but it was scaring the hell out of me. At one end of the room was what appeared to be a stone altar, and next to it a kind of baptismal font.

"This is really freaking me out," said Elsa. "Let's get out and come back later with some proper lighting. With just the flashlight beam, it's making it even scarier."

"I know what you mean," said the technician. "The faces just seem to jump out at you."

I was glad they felt that way, as I felt exactly the same. "Okay. We'll close it up and put the linoleum back. So no-one else is likely to find the damn place during the conference. Once all the delegates have gone back home, we'll come back and have a proper look." I shone the flashlight on to my wrist and looked at my watch. "It's mid afternoon already. Professor Charles is going to be arriving soon."

"Okay. Let's come back next week," said Elsa. "But for now, I've got to get out of here."

We returned back through the doorway, up the steps and into the basement. We rolled the linoleum back down and moved some heavy boxes from the other side of the basement so as to block off that corner.

We went back up the stairs, and the technician went back to work, whilst me and Elsa went to my office in the Library. I closed the door behind us.

"What do you make of it?"

"Super creepy," she replied. "Seems Hollister was up to more than we thought he was."

"Not just orgies?"

"Doesn't look like it."

"I honestly don't know what to make of it. I knew he was meant to have been into all of the pagan stuff. But that…temple, or whatever it is. It's heavy shit. What did he use the altar for?"

"I don't like to think," she replied. "Are you going to mention it to the Professor?"

"I'm not going to mention it straight out, but I might try and get him to say something."

"See if he offers any information?"

"Yeah."

"You don't think they know about it do you?"

"The College? If they do, they never mentioned it to me when I was shown around when I first started."

"So it could have remained unopened from when Hollister died to when the technician and Decker found it a few years ago."

"It's possible. Anything's possible. Let's just keep quiet about it for now."

"I think that's best."

"Good," I said, as I threw another log on the fire, suddenly feeling cold again. Just as I was about to sit down in the chair, the buzzer on the front gate video entry phone sounded. Elsa answered, said a few words and pushed the gate release button.

"Professor Charles?" I asked

"Yes," she said. "Let's go and meet him."

We headed for the front door.

I watched Professor Charles get out of the passenger side of a Ford E series van, and he walked over to me with a large smile on his face and his hand outstretched. "How nice to see you again Dominic."

"You too." I replied. "What's with the van. You moving in?"

"No. Not at all. I've just brought rather a lot of luggage and some things we need for the conference. You don't mind giving the driver a hand do you. I'm getting a bit old to be lifting heavy boxes."

"No don't mind at all," I said, "But first let me introduce you to Elsa Morales."

"Ah yes. Miss Morales. The new Housekeeper for the conference. How lovely to meet you."

"Hello Professor. It's nice to meet you to," replied Elsa. "Please come in. It's still a bit chilly. Even though it's meant to be Springtime now."

"Yes, it is, isn't it?" said Professor Charles. "My favourite time of year. In Spring a young man's fancy lightly turns to thought of love."

Me and Elsa looked at each knowingly and smiled. "Couldn't have put it better myself," I said. "Who was that. Keats?"

"Tennyson."

"I knew it was one of those English guys," I said, and I gestured that I would go and unload the van.

Me and the driver carried three large trunks into the lodge and put them down on the hallway floor. "Where do you want these?" I asked.

"Please put this one one in the Ballroom, where the conference will be held," he pointed to one of the trunks. "And the other two in the basement please."

"The basement?"

"Yes. There's not a problem with that is there?" he said, looking suddenly concerned.

"No problem. No," I replied. "I just thought it would be easier to keep them up here. "The basement steps are quite steep."

"Don't worry Dominic," replied the Professor "We always keep them in the basement."

I nodded to the driver and we both carried them down.

Once I'd got back upstairs I tipped the driver and he left. Elsa and Professor Charles had made themselves comfortable by the fire in the Library.

"Would you like a drink?" I asked him.

"I'd love a brandy, if you have any," he replied.

"Yeah. I've got some Cognac somewhere. You too, Elsa?"

"Why not. Just a small one. Or I won't feel like doing any work later."

I poured us three brandies, handed out the glasses, and we toasted the success of the conference.

"How are you getting on at Eagle Creek, Dominic?" asked the Professor.

"It's great. And certainly different. Hollister must have been quite a guy."

"He certainly was," replied the Professor. "I suppose by today's reckoning he would have been a billionaire. Very successful businessman. And a major art and antiquities collector."

"All from Hollister's Corned Beef," I said.

"That was the foundation of his wealth, but he'd expanded into many other areas as well. Real Estate, railways, shipping."

"What got him so interested in antiquities?" asked Elsa, looking super cute sipping her Cognac, the liquor bringing a slight glow to her beautiful golden skin.

"He studied the ancient world at Marlow, and he was always fascinated by it. In fact it was him that started the conferences at Eagle Creek."

"So there were conferences when he was still alive? Before he left the lodge to the College endowment?"

"Sort of, yes. Although they weren't really called conferences. They were a gathering of various academics and experts. It was more informal," explained the Professor. "Then after he died, the College decided to set up the conferences in memory of him. At first they were just once every five years. But in the late sixties they became an annual event and then about twenty years ago they became twice yearly."

"What kind of things do you discuss?" asked Elsa.

"Fairly obscure subjects, I'm afraid. For instance, we have a lecture this year on the 'Funerary Practises of the Canaanites', and another on the "Sacred Art of the Hittites'."

"So that's why you wanted the Canaanite goddess sculpture," I said.

"Yes Dominic. Have you finished her?"

"She's more or less done. Do you want to see?"

"Absolutely. I'd love to," he replied.

"She's in my studio," I said, and they followed me out of the library.

We entered the studio and I turned on the lights. Professor Charles went over to the sculpture, and ran his hands along it, examining it from every angle. "It's wonderful Dominic. Everything I hoped it would be. I knew you were the man for the job, when I first saw your work. Splendid. She is absolutely magnificent. Beautiful."

"I guess you like it then."

"Couldn't be bettered. Even the goddess herself will feel honoured."

"What are you going to do with her?"

"Can you take her through to the Ballroom?"

"Yes. I can get one of the porters to help me tomorrow morning. They'll be in to finish the conference preparations."

"Good. The other delegates will love her too, I'm sure."

"You are a modern day genius Dominic. And you Miss Morales, you're very lucky to have such a talented partner."

"Partner?"

"I believe partner is the modern word for it, yes," replied the Professor, the corner of his lip curling into an enigmatic smile.

"I'm not sure I…" said Elsa.

"Don't be shy Miss Morales. It is Spring time after all," he said. "And I think I'll take a lie down for a few hours. The altitude of Steamy Springs always seems to affect me the first day I arrive."

"Of course," I said. "I'll show you your room."

"That won't be necessary. Is it the one I stipulated?"

"Yes."

"Then I'll see you for supper later," he said, and he left my studio and headed upstairs.

I saw the look on Elsa's face and knew what she was thinking. "Well?"

"How does he know about us?"

"I have no idea. He's a wily old fox. He must have caught me looking at you."

"Well at least it's out in the open, I suppose."

"That's one way of looking at it. Anyway you don't want to hide it, do you?"

"No. I'm just amazed that he knew. You didn't want to keep it quiet?"

"Me? No. I want to shout it from the rooftops. I don't care if the whole world knows."

Elsa snuggled up to my chest and I put my arm around her and kissed her on the top of her head. "Let's just make it through the next few days and then we've got the house to ourselves again for the next six months."

"Just the two of us is good. But I'm not sure I want to live here. There's something about this place which is giving me bad vibes."

"You still thinking about the vault."

"Yes."

"Don't worry. It's just some weird room that Hollister played at being an ancient Roman in." Unfortunately, I didn't really believe that myself. The vault had really spooked me, and I also had a bad feeling in the pit of my stomach that not even the company of a beautiful girl and a glass of finest Cognac could shift.

Chapter 7

Friday arrived, and so did the delegates. The Airport bus pulled up outside the Lodge and me and the driver and one of the porters spent an hour carrying luggage upstairs, whilst Elsa showed the guests to their rooms.

There were twenty eight in total, including Professor Charles. Fourteen men and Fourteen women. Fourteen Americans, six Brits, four Canadians, two Germans, one French, and one Israeli. They were mostly middle aged, with a few a bit older, and one or two probably in their mid thirties.

By early afternoon they were all settled in, and I'd been rushed off my feet for the last six hours. Me and Elsa took a walk to get some fresh air and some privacy. I led her through the fields and up to the forestry. It was a good chance for her to see the estate, and it also allowed me to take a look at what Brockley had been doing. I suspected he was felling lots of trees and generally managing the forest irresponsibly. I was fairly sure he was more interested in short term profit than conserving it for the future.

"What do you think of the delegates?" I asked Elsa.

"They seem okay. Just a bunch of academics."

"Yeah."

"Where are you taking me, by the way?"

"Just up to the forest."

"Why?"

"I want to have a look around. And, because you haven't seen it before."

"Is it something special?"

"It's just a forest, I guess. Nothing unusual."

"There's nothing dangerous there is there?"

"Like what?"

"Bears, wolves, snakes."

"I doubt it. It's not really wilderness. It's a managed part of the Estate. If there are any snakes, I doubt we'll see them."

"Why doesn't that re-assure me?"

"If we do see one, just run like crazy."

"You scared of them?"

"Never seen one, except in a zoo. But I don't like them."

"Is this it?" said Elsa, pointing to the tree line just in front of us.

"This is the start of it, yes." I said, and I bent down and picked up a small branch from the ground.

"What's that for?"

"Nothing. Just like to pick something up when I'm walking. A stick. It's a man thing."

"For sure."

We walked around inside the woodland for a while, looking at the various types of trees and poking around in the undergrowth with my stick.

"What's that over there?" said Elsa.

"Where?"

"That vehicle."

I followed the direction her finger was pointing in, and saw what she was looking at. We walked up to it.

"It's a mechanical digger of some sort," I said. "Must be Brockley's. I guess he's using it to dig holes to plant the young trees in."

"I don't see any new trees, do you?"

"Not in this part. Maybe he's just starting here."

"There's a big hole over there."

I wandered over to have a look. There was a large trench, about the length and width of an SUV, and about ten feet deep. Stacked near the side of the trench were ten sacks of fertilizer.

"That's the stuff I sent back to the warehouse a few days ago."

"The stuff he shouldn't be using?"

"I knew he was doing something. I'll have to go and see him again after the conference."

"What's he using it for?"

"Must be trying to grow something here."

"People don't grow things in the forest, except trees. You don't think he's growing marijuana do you?"

"Not in the forest. I don't think so."

"Weird, huh?"

I took a closer look at the sacks. Potassium Hydroxide flakes.

"Brockley's a pain in the ass," I said, and kicked one of the sacks. "Come on. Let's go home. We've got a lot to do."

We returned to the Lodge, me silently cursing Brockley all the way back.

We'd been invited to have a few drinks with the delegates in the evening, and when we got back we showered and dressed and went downstairs to the Orangery where people were gathered and busy chatting. When we walked in, the conversation stopped and everyone turned to look at us. I put on a big smile and took a deep breath. I didn't really like these occasions, being with a group of people I didn't know, and I made a quick beeline for the drinks and got myself and Elsa a glass of wine.

Professor Charles took it upon himself to properly introduce us. "You will have seen Dominic and Elsa earlier, when you arrived. They are our new lodge Manager and Housekeeper, and so I'd just like to introduce you to them formally. Dominic and Elsa, welcome." He raised his glass, and everyone else did the same.

Me and Elsa were a little embarrassed at the attention and were glad when the individual conversations started up again, and the room was filled with chatter.

We were left talking to a Dr Harrison of London University, and who spent the next half hour telling us about his work studying burial artefacts from the ancient near east. Fascinating in a way, and certainly more interesting once you had a glass, or two, or three, of wine.

The evening passed fairly quickly and without any real event. By the time me and Elsa decided to leave we'd worked our way around most of the people in the room, and they had all been pretty much as we had expected. Polite, softly spoken, intellectual, passionate about their individual subjects, a few bores, a handful of borderline alcoholics, but no outright crazies or sociopaths.

We went up to bed, and shut the door behind us, relieved to be alone together. We got into bed, snuggled up to each other and watched TV for a while. There was an old British horror movie on a cable channel, about some bright young things stumbling across a creepy old house, where the owner's cannibal son lived in a secret room in the attic. It was called *The Ghoul*. It was enjoyable enough, but both me and Elsa kept our fears to ourselves about things like hidden rooms, and what might be lurking in them.

We put the light off and made love for the next hour, finding joy and comfort in each other, before drifting off to sleep around midnight.

Chapter 8

Saturday morning was hectic, managing temporary staff, preparing and clearing breakfast, getting things ready for lunch, and for the big dinner in the evening.

The conference was under way in the ballroom, with the only apparent sign that anything was happening, being the faintly audible sound of a film showing on the big screen that had been set up. I listened with my ear against the door a few times, but I couldn't really make out what they were talking about. The door was about eight inch thick solid wood, and virtually no sound or light could penetrate it. They were sealed in the room, in their own little world.

After breakfast, I'd gone over the plan for the day with Professor Charles. The conference sessions would end at four, and the delegates would then go and get ready for the evening dinner, which was to start at six-thirty. Me and Elsa had an hour to put away a lot of the equipment, shift the big conference table to the end of the room, cover it in a large velvet cloth, and lay out the buffet meal on it. After that, Professor Charles and some other delegates would continue to prepare the room. Me and Elsa were asked to stay in the Library for the rest of the evening and, should we be needed, someone would come and knock on the door. All other temporary staff were to have left the house by four o' clock, and I wasn't to allow anyone else in. There were to be no interruptions tonight.

It all seemed to be a bit over the top, but they were paying my bills, so I went along with it. At four, the conference broke up for the day and they all seemed to return quickly to their rooms. Me and Elsa dashed in and carried out Professor Charles's instructions to the letter.

The room looked pretty good. Whatever they were going to be doing, they couldn't complain about the spread of food we'd laid on for them, and I was particularly pleased to see that my sculpture took pride of place at the opposite end of the room to the buffet, up on a little raised stage area.

We took one final look around. Elsa polished wine glasses and I re-arranged some fruit in to what I thought looked like a more artistic arrangement. We then left, went to the library and closed the door behind us.

We'd kept some food for ourselves and had a good stock of drinks. The log fire was burning merrily, and we sat down in front of it, putting our feet up for a while.

At five-thirty, Professor Charles came into the room and brought us a gift of a bottle of wine. "This is for all your help today he said, and he went over to the side table and opened it for us. "Enjoy. It's from one of the finest Bordeaux estates. Very rare. Very expensive."

He reminded us not to disturb them and then pulled the door shut. I then heard the sound of a key turning. I went over to the door and tried to open it. It was locked .

"I can't believe they locked us in," I said, feeling pissed off. "I'm not that interested in seeing what they're doing."

"Yes you are."

"Okay. I admit I am."

"Guess, we're prisoners in here for the next five or six hours, then," said Elsa.

"Looks like it."

"Do you think they're having some kind of orgy?"

"That's exactly what I think. Did you count the numbers. Fourteen men, fourteen women. Couples. They're having one huge swingers party in there."

"You really think so?"

"Yeah. Why else would they be so secretive?"

"I didn't realise these academic types were into that sort of thing."

"Neither did I. But I can't really think of any other explanation. Whatever it is, I bet it includes them being naked and worshipping the goddess. Some weird shit like that."

I poured us both a large glass of red wine, and took a mouthful. I turned on the TV to see if there was anything worth watching. We sat for a while, drinking wine, nibbling at the canapes, and happily watching a re-run of a forensics drama. I was getting quite interested in the story. The team were investigating a case where some mobsters had disposed of a dead body in the hills, burying it, and covering it in lime in the mistaken belief that it would decompose the body. What it actually did was preserve the body.

My mind was suddenly troubled by a thought, something forming in the back of my mind, but not yet clear enough to know exactly what my sub-conscious was trying to tell me. I was nicely relaxed from the wine, and the two halves of my brain were fighting over whether to think further about it, or just sit back and enjoy the show. I looked at Elsa next to me and saw that she'd fallen asleep. I thought it must have been the combination of a busy day, the wine, and the warm fire we were sitting next to. I got up to pour myself another glass, and I suddenly felt very light-headed. I looked at the bottle on the table in front of me and my vision started to blur. My limbs felt heavy, a sense of panic ran through me, and I knew I was going to faint. I staggered towards the wall to try and lean on something. I took some deep breaths and tried to steady myself. It was no good. I was going down. The last thing I remember I was falling towards the floor. And then, everything went black.

Chapter 9

I woke up sometime later to find myself lying in a strange room, staring up at the ceiling. I felt a little groggy and my eyes strained to to see what was going on. As soon as my mind had begun to clear, my lassitude was replaced by fear. I was in the vault under the lodge. It was dimly lit by candlelight, and my hands were strapped down to the stone altar. I was naked. I looked to the side of me and saw Elsa. She had been tied down too, and she was beginning to wake up All around us I was aware of people wearing hooded cloaks, with their faces covered by white masks. Was I dreaming this? Was this some dreadful nightmare?

I tried to free my hands but the strap wouldn't give at all. I thrashed my legs, but there was nowhere for them to connect with, and the position I was in meant I was unable to stand up.

Suddenly, the people around me started to chant in a strange, rhythmic way, gradually getting louder and faster, as they joined hands and spun in a circle around the altar.

This continued for several minutes, and I was now wide awake, and almost paralysed with fear. I looked at Elsa again, and this time she looked back at me. Her eyes filled with terror. I wanted to speak, but I had no idea what to say. *Don't worry* or *Are you okay?* hardly seemed to be appropriate under the circumstances. Of course she wasn't okay, she was strapped naked to an altar, the centrepiece of some utterly insane pagan religious ritual. Of course she was going to fucking worry. I was fucking shitting myself. I let out an involuntary laugh at the situation I was in. I don't know if I was going crazy, or if laughter seemed like the only appropriate thing to do.

Then the chanting stopped, and a hooded figure stood in front of me. And as if things couldn't get worse, he was holding a long, very sharp looking knife. I guessed he wasn't here to cut me free from the straps. My stomach turned over a few times and I felt sick. I couldn't see a way out of this. I looked at Elsa again. She was crying, and I nodded at her, hoping that my eyes would convey how much I loved her. I stretched out my fingers and I realised that if she did the same we could just about touch each other. Perhaps the last thing we could do was offer each other the simple comfort of touch. If this was it. If I was going to die tonight, I wanted to do it with Elsa by my side. We looked into each other's eyes, as if to say goodbye, and see you on the other side if there's anything there. I wasn't especially religious, but I'd had a typical Italian Catholic upbringing. Enough, that it got me to wondering whether there was another world after this.

The masked figure in front of me lifted the knife high above his head and loomed over me menacingly. The chanting started up again and he returned to the circle, which began to rotate around us again. I guessed the fucker with the knife was Professor Charles, and I wondered how many times he was going to spin around the altar before he laid into me with the knife. Or did they all have knives? Were we going to be ripped to shreds by these lunatics?

They say that at the end, your thinking becomes real clear and sharp. Lucid. I didn't know if that was true, but everything that had happened to me since I was first offered the job suddenly became Grade A fucking crystal clear. None of it was an accident. I'd been set up from the beginning. They'd picked me out as a human sacrifice the moment they'd first seen me. Elsa too. Her boss had connections at Marlow, she'd said. He was in on it as well. Making the goddess sculpture. What was I fucking thinking? Hollister, the pagan motifs throughout the house, the vault I was now in, the secret conference sessions, the fertility rites, the couples who'd gone missing from Steamy Springs every Spring and Autumn, Decker's disappearance. It all made sense now. I might not have had any clear idea where my soul was going after death, but I sure as hell knew where my body was going tonight. Into the fucking pit Brockley had dug in the forest. Covered in chemicals to throw the police dogs off the scent, and make sure we decompose quicker. No doubt Decker and his wife were there somewhere as well, fertilizing the trees that had been planted on top of them. How could I have been so fucking stupid?

The crazies were doing some kind of weird dance now. No doubt full of symbolism and meaning. But if they thought I was going to appreciate it, they were out of their fucking minds. Me and Elsa were just about to get our asses cut off , and they were doing the freakin' samba. My fear was now being replaced by anger. Strategically, I was shifting from defense to offense.

Whilst they were busy spinning and gyrating, I gestured to Elsa to stretch her fingers as much as she could and try and loosen the strap that was holding my wrist down to the altar. I felt sure if she could just manage to undo the buckle I could get out. Once I had one hand free, I'd be in with a chance. She immediately understood what I wanted her to do, and she made an effort to pull the leather strap. Luckily the room was so dimly lit that they wouldn't see what we were trying to do. Her nimble fingers worked on the strap and she just about managed to pull it through the buckle. Another inch and she could undo it properly. She tried again and this time it came. My hand was free.

The chanting stopped. The masked man returned to the altar, the candlelight gleaming on the curved blade of the knife. He stood over me and raised the knife once more. The others began to chant strange words over and over again, as if willing him onwards. They were eager for blood.

It was now or never. Just as he was about to plunge the knife, I pulled my hand from the strap, lifted myself off of the altar and swung my fist towards his masked face. "You want blood. Taste some of your own, fucker," I shouted.

My fist slammed into his face, and he reeled backwards. I quickly undid the other strap, and jumped to my feet. It all happened so quickly the other members of the cult barely knew what was happening. I wrestled the knife from the man, and tore the mask from his face. It was Professor Charles. I punched him again, right on the nose, and I heard it shatter. He fell to the ground.

I freed Elsa from the altar, and we both stood behind it facing twenty-seven masked people on the other side Our only advantage was the knife I was holding. Professor Charles started to stir and I hit him in the face again with a sharp reverse kick of my heel.

My eyes darted around the room, looking for an escape. I grabbed a candle from a stone shelf behind me. I told Elsa to remove professor Charles's cloak, and she tore it from his body. The other crazies were now starting to close in on us. I held the candle up to the cloak and watched as it started to smoke. A second later it burst into flames and I threw it over two of the others who were closest to us. It landed on their heads and one of them quickly caught fire. The vault erupted in panic as the other cult members tried to extinguish the flames.

This was our chance. I grabbed Elsa's hand and we ran for the doorway. I barged another one of them out of the way, flooring him with a head butt. We made it through and sprinted up the steps. They were right behind us, only inches from our heels. We leapt through the trapdoor and into the basement. I slammed the stone door down, catching someone's fingers in it. They screamed like a wounded animal. I picked it up and slammed it down again. Another scream. Once more. And this time they removed their hand, and I was able to close it properly. I rolled the linoleum back and pushed a couple of Professor Charles's heavy travel trunks over the entrance. I made double sure by pushing an old desk over it as well. I was covinced they wouldn't get out, unless there was another exit.

Elsa and me ran out of the cellar and locked the door behind us. We went to the library, found our clothes. Pulled on jeans and T-shirts, grabbed my keys and cellphone and we hurried to the SUV.

I started the engine, and kept it revving. Elsa phoned 911, and the Police said they'd be there in five minutes.

"Are we going?" said Elsa.

"I think we're OK. The Police will be here any minute."

"Can they get out of the vault?"

"I doubt it."

"I'm scared Nic. Let's just go."

"Okay. We'll wait outside the main gate," I said, as I put the SUV in gear and put my foot down, only then realizing that I wasn't wearing any shoes.

As I sped down the long driveway towards the gate I noticed headlights in my rear view mirror. There was someone chasing after us. How the hell had they got out?

I pressed the electronic gate opener, hoping that it would swing open in time. I was hitting ninety now, and if we smashed into the big iron gates, we'd be mangled. The vehicle behind us was virtually tailgating us now. They were trying to knock us off the driveway and into the trees at the side. The gate was now in site, and it was half way open. I tugged my seat belt on and shouted to Elsa to do the same. I clicked the gate control again. This time closing it. Now on the final straight towards the gate, only fifty feet to go, I braked sharply and swerved the SUV off the driveway and onto the grass verge. Whoever was driving the truck behind hadn't expected my manoeuvre, and by the time they had realised what I was doing it was too late. The truck smashed into the gates, tore them from their hinges, careered across the highway that passed by the lodge and crashed into a tree, where it came to a stop.

Surprised that we'd survived our high speed turn, I gunned the engine again, headed for the gateway and pulled out onto the highway. I stopped the SUV and took off my seatbelt.

"Where are you going?"

"Just going to see who it is."

"Let's just go to town."

"I'll be ten seconds." I jumped out and ran over to the crashed truck. It was totally smashed up. Whoever was driving wouldn't have survived. I peered in through what remained of the side window. His head was splattered over the windshield. It was Brockley.

As I ran back to the SUV, I heard the sirens and saw the flashing lights of five or six Police vehicles approaching from just over the hill. I got in and took hold of Elsa's hand. "We're okay now, honey. We're okay."

Chapter 10

Me and Elsa sat in the kitchen at Eagle Creek sipping coffee and reading the newspapers. A nice, leisurely Saturday morning. The front pages were full of the news of the trial of the cult members. It was almost certain they were going down for life imprisonment. It had been six months now since we'd almost been their next victims, and there hadn't been a day since I hadn't said a little prayer of thanks to whichever guardian angel had been on our side that night.

It had taken us a few weeks before we'd wanted to even go back to Eagle Creek alone. I went with the Sheriff's men a few times to talk them over what had happened, but I still felt a little uneasy, as if some masked man was going to jump out at me. But gradually, we got over it, and we're both living at Eagle Creek full time, because I now own it. Marlow College were so shocked at what had happened that they signed over the house to me if I wanted it, along with a big fat cheque that's set us up for life. I'd considered a lawsuit, but I figured the lawyers would drag it out for years and end up taking most of the money for themselves. I was happy with the house and financial settlement offered by Marlow.

The publicity also did my career the world of good. My work has been selling to collectors and galleries all over the country, and I even managed to get six figures for the Astarte sculpture.

Me and Elsa are enjoying our life together in Steamy Springs, and I've no plans to leave. I like it here. The experience of that night brought us real close, and apart from the odd nightmare, we're now just about fully recovered from the ordeal.

On taking possession of the house, our first act was to get rid of a lot of the pagan stuff. That brought in a nice sum at auction, as well. I kept the mosaics in the spa room, because they're kind of fun, and me and Elsa have had some good times in there. As for the vault, I don't yet know what to do with it. Part of me wants to keep it as it is, the other part is considering hiring contractors to pump concrete into it. We'll see.

I took another bite of toast and made another drink. "You want more coffee, Honey"

"Please. And can you pass me that magazine over there?"

I glanced at it, and handed it to her. She took it, and we both smiled at each other. I continued to read about the trial, and Elsa opened up her copy of *Bride* magazine. Life was pretty good.